HEARTSIDE BAY

THE **HEARTSIDE BAY** SERIES

1. The New Girl

2. The Trouble With Love

3. More Than a Love Song

4. A Date With Fate

5. Never a Perfect Moment

6. Kiss at Midnight

7. Back to You

8. Summer of Secrets

9. Playing the Game

10. Flirting With Danger

11. Lovers and Losers

12. Winter Wonderland

HEARTSIDE BAY

The Trouble With Love

CATHY COLE

■SCHOLASTIC

First published in 2014 by Scholastic Children's Books
An imprint of Scholastic Ltd
Euston House, 24 Eversholt Street, London, NW1 1DB, UK
Registered office: Westfield Road, Southam, Warwickshire, CV47 0RA
SCHOLASTIC and associated logos are trademarks and/or
registered trademarks of Scholastic Inc.

Text copyright © Scholastic Ltd, 2014

ISBN 978 1407 14047 6

A CIP catalogue record for this book
is available from the British Library.

Printed by CPI Group (UK) Ltd, Croydon, CR0 4YY
Papers used by Scholastic Children's Books are made
from wood grown in sustainable forests.

1 3 5 7 9 10 8 6 4 2

This is a work of fiction. Names, characters, places, incidents
and dialogues are products of the author's imagination or are used
fictitiously. Any resemblance to actual people, living or dead,
events or locales is entirely coincidental.

www.scholastic.co.uk

Big thanks to Lucy Courtenay
and Sara Grant

ONE

Polly Nelson couldn't take her eyes off the stitching along the hem of the flowy skirt she was wearing. She had chosen it so carefully that afternoon. She couldn't believe she'd left the house in something that looked so bad.

The campfire crackled merrily, the smell of toasting marshmallows mingling with the salty beach air, the pumping bass from Max's MP3 and the lively sound of chatter. It was surprisingly warm for a February afternoon, even without the fire. Polly tucked the offending skirt under her legs, hoping that she wouldn't think about it so much that way. She looked terrible. She hoped no one would notice.

On the opposite side of the fire, Polly's best friend

Lila Murray had finished threading her stick with marshmallows and was placing them in the flames. Her glossy brown hair was whipped up by the wind coming in from the sea, and she was laughing at something her boyfriend Ollie Wright was saying. She was so pretty, Polly thought, and had such infectious enthusiasm for everything. No wonder Ollie was mad about her. It was hard to believe Lila had only come to Heartside Bay a few weeks ago. It felt like they'd known each other for half their lives.

It's half-term, Polly scolded herself. *You're in the secret cove with your friends, a bonfire, marshmallows and great music. What's not to like?*

This skirt looks awful, her thoughts replied at once.

What are you going to do about it? Polly challenged herself. *Take it off and dance around the beach in your underwear?*

Her gaze flickered towards Ollie. He looked extra-gorgeous when he laughed, she thought wistfully.

She'd had a secret crush on Ollie since her first day at Heartside High. He had dropped a pencil by her feet in Year Eight, and she had kept it. She had written in detail about him in her diary in Year Nine, and treasured every private conversation they had ever had. After all these years, she still couldn't stop her heart from fluttering every time she saw him. And now he was Lila's.

As she gazed at Ollie, Polly caught Lila's eye. She instantly felt guilty. Did the fact that she fancied her best friend's boyfriend show in her face? Her wide hazel eyes were much too expressive, she knew. She loosed her hair and let it swing round her face like a thick black curtain.

"Half-term at last," Lila sighed happily. She fiddled with her marshmallow stick. "I can't believe it's here. We're going to have *so* much fun."

Polly felt a wave of relief. Lila hadn't read anything in her expression. It looked like her complicated feelings for Ollie were still a secret.

Ollie dusted sand off his jeans and snuggled his arm round Lila's shoulders. "And it starts right here," he said. "Are my marshmallows done yet?"

Lila guarded her marshmallow stick, baring her teeth like a dog. "Cook your own!" she warned, smiling.

"What's yours is mine," Ollie said innocently. "That's the way relationships work."

Lila kicked him with one bare, sandy foot. "You wish!"

Ollie launched himself at Lila, tickling her until she begged, squealing, for mercy. Then he cut off her laughter with a kiss.

Polly suddenly felt more lonely than she'd ever felt in her life.

"I'm going for a paddle," she said, getting up.

"Want some company?" Lila said, pushing Ollie off and raising herself up on her elbows. The sand in her hair made her look like an off-duty mermaid.

Polly shook her head. "Save a marshmallow for me?"

"Of course, Pol," Lila said warmly.

"Hey!" Ollie said in a mock-indignant voice. "You're letting her have one, but not me?"

Lila and Ollie were the perfect couple, Polly thought with a sigh as she took off her shoes and moved away from the campfire. They were both gorgeous, and bubbly, and popular. It had taken Lila a few weeks to settle in to her new school – thanks mainly to queen bee Eve Somerstown causing trouble – but now she was in the middle of every social event in Heartside and almost more popular than Eve herself. Lila had long legs, a rich laugh and beautiful thick brown hair. Why would Ollie look at anyone else – least of all, Polly?

Enough with this obsession, she thought, straightening her shoulders. It was time to move on. Anyway, Ollie represented everything she despised in boys. Dumb sexist humour, never taking anything seriously, and only ever thinking about football. He was wrong for her in every way.

There must be someone better out there for you, she consoled herself. *Someone more intelligent than Ollie, more sensitive, less sporty. Maybe with deep political convictions. Now* that *would be a dream boy.*

She reached the edge of the sea and let the cold waves swish over her toes. The sea always calmed her down and helped her to think more clearly. She couldn't imagine living inland. It would be torture, knowing that the ocean was curling and crashing over someone else's feet, not her own.

Polly glanced over her shoulder at the sound of laughter. Rhi and Eve were chasing Rhi's boyfriend Max down the beach, throwing handfuls of sand after him. Max ran backwards, grinning and waving as Rhi and Eve chased him. His dark curly hair blew around his head.

"Catch me if you can!" he whooped teasingly.

"Oh, we'll catch you!" Eve shouted. "Don't worry about that, Max!"

"No one eats our marshmallows and gets away with it!" Rhi added, gasping with laughter as she flung her sand in Max's direction. It fell harmlessly by his feet.

"Typical girl," Max taunted with a grin, racing back towards the campfire. "Can't throw to save your life!"

Why can't I be more like Eve? Polly thought, watching them. *Totally comfortable hanging out with her best friend and her boyfriend?*

She shook her head, surprised at herself. She could never be like Eve in any way. Eve made everyone's lives a misery. Lila had been through hell in her first couple of weeks at Heartside High because of Eve. She had made Polly's life miserable too. Eve was as trustworthy as a snake.

Polly watched as Eve, true to form, threw herself beside the others by the campfire, accidentally on purpose knocking Lila's arm and spilling her water in her lap.

"Whoops," she drawled, not sounding in the least bit sorry.

"Whoops yourself," Lila said, and dumped what was left of her water over Eve's head.

"Ugh!"

Eve jumped furiously to her feet, mopping hard at her cashmere jumper. Rhi helped her to dry off the worst of the water with Max's help. Ollie just laughed.

"I'm really sorry, Eve," said Lila with an innocent-looking shrug. "It was a total mistake. My hand has a life of its own, didn't you know?"

Even from a distance, Polly could see Eve's eyes were glittering with rage.

"That wasn't kind, Lila," said Rhi reproachfully.

"She did it to me first," Lila pointed out, wiping herself dry. "You have to learn to take what you dish out, Eve. Just be glad I wasn't drinking anything sticky."

"I spilled your drink by *accident*," Eve hissed.

"Funny kind of accident," said Lila, rolling her eyes. "You have to stop with all these silly games, Eve. We're all tired of your behaviour."

"Give it a rest, will you?" said Max lazily, swiping a marshmallow. "This is supposed to be a party."

"I will not," Eve snapped, and jumped to her feet. "She started it."

Several of the other girls in their class rallied round Eve with Rhi and Max. Lila stood up warily, with Ollie, a group of Ollie's footballing mates and a bunch of other kids clustered round her in support.

Polly felt nervous. Things had been extra tense between Lila and Eve since Valentine's Day. It was great that Lila wasn't putting up with Eve's tricks any more, but things were getting out of hand.

It was beginning to feel like the whole school was split between supporters of Eve and supporters of Lila. The tension was awful. It wasn't the best way to start half-term.

"Fight!" someone yelled.

TWO

The groups swelled and pushed at each other. Polly started running, back to the fire.

"Stop!" she shouted. "Don't fight, please don't fight!" She threw herself between the two groups. "Don't do this," she begged, waving her arms for calm. "It's half-term! We're supposed to enjoy ourselves, not start a war."

Eve gave Lila a furious icy stare. "*She* can't get away with a stunt like that."

Lila glared back, hands on her hips. "And *she* needs to pull her head out of her own—"

Eve rushed at Lila before she could finish, hands raised and nails poised to strike. Polly stumbled backwards. Ollie leapt between Eve and Lila as Eve tried to scratch Lila's face. Amid the yelling, pushing and shoving, someone yelped in pain as they trod in the smouldering remains of the campfire, squishing marshmallows into the sand.

Polly could feel anxiety racing through her body. She could feel her lungs squeezing up, not giving her enough oxygen.

"No!" she panted, and grabbed the arm of the nearest person, pulling them backwards.

"Hey!" Ollie said, pulled off-balance as he staggered against her.

Polly's body gave a shiver of pleasure at the sensation of Ollie right up against her skin. *Imagine these arms around you*, she thought, feeling a little dizzy. *Nothing could ever hurt you.*

"Please stop this, Ollie," she begged, forcing her thoughts back to reality. "There are better ways to solve conflict than fighting like idiots."

"Not everyone's as perfect as you," he said angrily, shaking her hand off. "Now isn't the time for *talking*."

Polly hit back with the only thing she could think of. "Of course, the concept of talking is beyond your little brain, isn't it, Ollie? The only things inside your head are Lila and football . . . and . . . and marshmallows. Your brain is *made* of marshmallows!"

He stepped backwards. She winced at the hurt in his eyes.

"Get back to your dictionaries, Little Miss Perfect," he snapped. "OK, so I play football. That doesn't mean I'm dumb. It's not like you never make mistakes." He scanned her skirt. "That outfit, for instance. You look like one of those stupid Spanish dolls that tourists buy on holiday."

Polly felt utterly crushed.

Great work, she told herself. *Get the guy you like to really hate you.* She knew the skirt was a bad idea. Now it seemed to be laughing at her.

"When I need fashion advice, I know who to turn to," she said, trying to stop her voice from wobbling. It was all she could do not to run away from the beach, away from everyone, and just keep running until she got home and changed and forgot everything about this horrible afternoon.

Ollie's eyes flickered. "Back off, Polly. And don't stick your nose where it isn't wanted."

The two groups were slinking away now, eyeing

each other sourly. Eve had stormed off down the beach with Rhi and Max. Straightening her top and looking a little sheepish, Lila picked up her marshmallows from the blanket and offered them to Polly.

"That got a bit crazy, didn't it?" she said with a little laugh. "You can have the first marshmallow if you want, Pol. They're veggie ones."

Polly folded her arms tightly across her chest and shook her head. Ollie was still glaring at her. She wanted to disappear into the sand.

Lila seemed to notice the chilly atmosphere. "The fight's over, guys. Hadn't you noticed?" she said, her expression suddenly worried. "What's going on?"

"She told me I had a brain like a marshmallow," Ollie muttered.

Lila gave a snort of laughter. "Pink or white?"

Ollie gave a reluctant smile. "We didn't get as far as flavours," he said.

Lila flipped Polly a marshmallow and held out her arms for Ollie. Polly's heart broke a little more as Ollie went to give Lila a hug.

He's my best friend's boyfriend and a stupid jock, she reminded herself desperately. *Not my type at all. Not to mention the fact that he now hates me anyway.*

The marshmallow tasted of ashes as she slowly put it into her mouth.

The afternoon grew darker and the campfire brighter. Someone turned the music up and people started dancing on the sand, some pressed up close together and others swaying in their own little worlds. The cliffs of the secret cove curled around them, a half-moon of golden rocks, connected to the outside world by just two paths. Polly clutched her drink and tried to listen to what Liam was saying.

Liam was goalkeeper on the football team. Big and strong as an ox, his thick black hair stood up on his head like a startled hedgehog.

"Great skirt." Liam patted Polly's knee with a beefy hand more used to catching balls. He took a swig from his drink. "Very . . . skirty." He hiccupped and wiped the back of his hand across his lips. "Flirty skirty," he added, and grinned at her.

Liam wasn't particularly intelligent, but he wasn't horrible, or one of the louder footie idiots that clustered around Ollie. His clumsy attempt at flattery was sort of nice, only his breath smelled and there was a bright red spot on his nose. And he was a jock. Her least favourite kind of guy.

Stop overthinking things, Polly told herself impatiently. She always did this, working out a hundred reasons not to do something.

She wondered if she should kiss Liam. Her first kiss. What would it be like? Would she even know what to do? She was so embarrassed that she'd never kissed someone before. Liam obviously wanted to. Maybe if she pretended Liam was someone else. Someone tall and blond, with blue eyes and a big smile. . .

She felt Liam's massive arm creep round her shoulders.

"You're cute," he said, smiling hopefully. The spot on his nose shone like a beacon. "Like a little doll."

Polly froze as Ollie's cruel words flooded back.

You look like one of those stupid Spanish dolls that tourists buy on holiday.

She couldn't do this.

"Sorry," she said abruptly as Liam moved towards her for a kiss.

Scrambling to her feet, she ran away from the campfire towards the sea. She was shaking. How could she feel so much for someone who could say something so hurtful? She could still feel the press of Ollie's body against hers as she pulled him out of the fight. She was ashamed at how the memory made her feel.

Panic started to wash over her, as rhythmic and insistent as the sea by her feet. She could feel the world narrowing, as if the cliffs of the cove were about to close around her and squeeze her between their cold, rough edges.

Breathe, she told herself, feeling her chest tightening up. *You have to get this under control!*

The constant movement of the sea was starting to make her feel sick. The panic was rising like the tide. She looked around in desperation, trying to find something else to focus on and bring her thoughts to a safer place.

Her eyes settled on Max and Rhi, tucked away in a private little nook in the cliffs near the path to Heartside's main beach, their arms wrapped tightly around each other as they kissed.

What is it with romance in this place? she thought in despair.

It was as if Heartside Bay, capital of romance, made you love people whether you wanted to or not. Except no one loved her. All she wanted was to go home, take her stupid skirt off and throw it in the bin.

Polly started walking towards the path that would lead her back to the centre of town. She averted her eyes from the two heads, one dark and one auburn, that were kissing so intently in the cliff nook. Then she paused.

Rhi and Max both had dark hair.

Max wasn't kissing Rhi. He was kissing *Eve*.

Polly's heart thumped as Eve pulled back from Max – and caught Polly's eye.

A rush of colour flooded Eve's pale cheeks. "Spying, are you?" she accused, grabbing her coat and pulling it protectively around herself.

At first, Polly couldn't find the words to express her shock. "You. . . *traitor*!" she said at last. She looked with disgust at Max, who was scrambling behind Eve as if that would somehow hide his betrayal of Rhi.

"Run and tell Rhi then, why don't you?" Eve challenged.

The tremble in her voice proved Eve wasn't as cool

about being caught as she was trying to make out. Polly realized that she looked scared. Eve was never scared.

If I were Eve, Polly thought, *I'd run right to the campfire and tell everyone, not just Rhi. But I'm not Eve.*

Polly had problems of her own, and not just with her crush on Ollie. Her friends and family knew nothing about her anxieties, or the trouble she had controlling them. She couldn't face the idea of telling tales tonight.

"I hope you're both very happy together," she said coldly, and stormed away towards the main beach.

THREE

Polly approached the rocky outcrop at the very tip of Heartside Bay. Clambering over the rocks, slipping and sliding in the rockpools dotted with little starfish and crabs, gave her the chance to think about something that wasn't Eve, and wasn't Ollie, and wasn't any of the other nameless fears and worries that she struggled with every day. She was forced to concentrate on simply putting one foot in front of the other. It worked like a kind of therapy. By the time she reached the very last rock, she felt calm again.

Standing here is almost as good as being in the middle of the sea, Polly thought, and she breathed the damp salty air into her lungs.

How could Eve do something like that to Rhi?

The two girls had been best mates ever since Rhi had moved to Heartside. Everyone at school knew what Eve could be like, but Polly thought Eve would at least be loyal to her own friends. It seemed that she was wrong. And Max! Polly had always liked Max, with his ready smile, his sharp brain and the way he had seemed to care about Rhi. It looked as if Polly didn't know him either.

Her mind returned restlessly to Ollie again. Her dreams of Ollie were like the waves she was looking at, retreating and then crashing again and again against the rocks. Even the shock of Eve and Max's betrayal couldn't keep him out of her mind for long.

She gazed across the causeway towards Kissing Island, Heartside's most famous natural feature. The causeway was already partly covered by the tide. You could only ever reach the island when the tides were right.

Local legend claimed that if you kissed your true love on the shores of Kissing Island at midnight on a full moon, you would be together for ever. Even though Polly had only lived in Heartside Bay since she was nine, she couldn't remember a time when she hadn't known the legend. But she had never actually been to the island.

She was saving it for the right boy, she thought, resting her eyes on the island's familiar bumps and crags. But who was the right boy? Ollie? Or someone else, someone she had yet to meet?

She closed her eyes and let her mind drift into her favourite daydream.

She and Ollie were standing hand in hand on the shore of Kissing Island, the sand cool between their toes. The light from the full moon striped the shoreline and made the sea glitter.

Polly sighed as she imagined Ollie turning to her, tipping her face towards his.

"I love you, Polly. I always have. I hope this feeling lasts for ever."

In her imagination, she wrapped her arms around his broad back, sliding her hands along his muscular shoulders. A little sigh escaped from her lips as she pictured how his warmth and strength would feel beneath her fingers.

"I love you too, Ollie. I've dreamed of this moment for so long."

His lips would be cool and soft, pressing hesitantly against hers at first, and then harder as passion overwhelmed them. She could feel his fingers twining through her hair, and the sweet taste of his mouth. . .

"How could you?!"

Polly tried to hold on to her dream, but it was sliding away from her. Now Lila was striding towards them, her cheeks streaked with tears and her eyes wide and desolate.

"I thought you were my friend!"

Polly squeezed her eyes tightly shut. She could never do what Eve had done to Rhi. Never. And so Ollie could never be hers.

Sobs rose in her throat as the picture in her mind changed again. Everyone in her life had surrounded her now. They were pointing and laughing, or shaking their heads at her treachery . . . her bare-faced lies. . .

Her father's face was the worst of all. She imagined the tone of his voice.

"I'm so disappointed in you, Polly. . . I thought you were a better person than this. . ."

She wrenched her eyes open. The chance of her father ever coming to Heartside Bay, even to say such terrible things to her, was so remote that it was laughable. He didn't care enough to visit from the US, or even to call her. His disappointment would be an improvement on his near-total absence.

She suddenly became aware that the sky had grown darker. The sun was low, striping the grey clouds with gold. How long had she been standing here? The wind felt colder than it had earlier in the afternoon, and the sea that surrounded her was getting rough. She looked with alarm at the water lapping against the rocks she was standing on. It was a lot higher than she had realized.

Fear clawed her throat as she gazed at the water creeping over the rocks that lay between her and the mainland. How could she have been so stupid not to realize the tide was coming in?

Even as she watched, the water level rose again. The waves seemed to reach for her, stretching out to dash themselves against her toes. Giving a gasp, Polly scrambled higher up the rock. Her panic returned, and she could barely breathe. She couldn't get back to the shore the way she had come – the water had covered too much of the rocks. She couldn't swim to shore either, because the sea was getting rougher by the minute. She could be dashed against the exact same rocks she was standing on, and drown.

"Help!" she screamed. "Someone, help me!"

Her voice vanished on the wind. The beach behind her was empty. The clouds were hanging ever lower in the blackening sky.

Polly sat down, swamped with horror at the danger she suddenly found herself in. There was no escape. She was going to be swept out to sea!

FOUR

The sun was almost touching the horizon now. Shivering with cold and fear, Polly clutched her knees and watched the rising water with a kind of horrible fascination. Would drowning be quick? She thought about jumping in and swimming for the shore, but the jagged rocks looked sharp and the currents strong. She was doomed either way.

A small boat with a blue sail appeared around the edge of the cliff on Polly's right. Hope surged through her. If she could get the sailor's attention, she would be saved!

You're such a cliché, Polly Nelson, she told herself. She unfolded her numb legs and and got unsteadily to her feet. *The damsel in distress, too involved in a stupid daydream to notice the tide!* If she had half a brain, she would never have come out here on the outcrop at this time in the afternoon. She was hardly living up to the image she had of herself.

The boat was still some distance away. Polly could make out a single sailor at the helm.

"Over here!" She waved so hard at the little boat that she almost lost her balance. "Help!"

She had a horrible feeling the sailor hadn't seen her yet. He was sailing fast, and in another five minutes she would be out of view. *Maybe I should tear off my skirt and wave it in the air like a flag*, she thought wildly. It was so colourful, they would have to be blind to miss her. But the thought of being rescued in her underwear was worse than the idea of drowning.

Finally, the sailor suddenly lifted a hand and waved back. Slowly but surely, the boat began to tack in her direction, the sail furling and billowing in the changing wind. The relief almost made Polly lose her balance. She sat down before her wobbly legs tipped her into the sea.

The boat was close enough now for Polly to make out the name painted on its white hull: *Arctic Angel*.

And she realized with a lurch that it was being steered by the hottest guy she'd ever seen. He was around her own age, tall with short dark hair and strong arms that seemed to effortlessly pull ropes and turn the wheel at the same time, and he was wearing a well-worn jumper in a washed-out cherry colour that brought out his light tan. Even from a distance, his white smile stood out like a flashlight in his brown skin.

"Having a bit of trouble?"

His voice was cultured, with long lazy vowels that suggested an expensive education.

"I. . ." Polly could hear her voice squeaking like a bat. He was even better looking close-up, and he was getting closer all the time. "I'm a mermaid, actually," she managed. "I do this all the time. Sit on rocks and wait for the tide to wash me out to sea."

Now isn't the time for sarcastic jokes, she thought in anguish. She probably sounded like a total idiot. But it was too late. She'd said it now.

He brought the *Arctic Angel* round so that it was closer to Polly's rock. "Then I should probably leave you here," he said thoughtfully. The boat bobbed under his feet, but he stood on its deck as steadily as if he had been on land. "Or I might fall in love with you and you'll drag me down to meet your father, King Neptune, and when we're halfway there I'll remember that I'm not a fish and drown."

They had only exchanged a handful of words and already she was half in love. If this boy had been sailing *into* the sunset instead of away from it, she would have thought she had fallen into a Hollywood movie. She smoothed her skirt, remembering how awful it looked. She had to get a grip.

"I'm guessing this isn't a tail time of year?" he added, gazing at her very human feet.

The rim of the sun was touching the sea behind him. *He doesn't think I'm mad,* Polly realized slowly. *Just, maybe, kind of funny. Now what?*

Run with it, she answered herself. *It feels good.*

"We not allowed to change past sunset," she improvised. "The water gets too dark to see where we're going."

"You should mention waterproof head-torches to Neptune next time you see him," the boy advised seriously.

The thought of mermaids swimming along with

torches on their heads was brilliantly stupid. Polly stopped worrying about her skirt and burst out laughing.

"Let me help you ashore, fish girl," he grinned.

Polly looked at the brown hand held out towards her. If she pinched herself, would he disappear? He was much too good to be true.

"Thank you, sailor boy," she said.

She would step purposefully and steadily on to the boat, then maybe stumble very slightly over a coil of rope lying on the deck and tip into his arms. She would apologize and he would tell her not to worry about it. They would gaze into each other's eyes. . .

"Can't you reach me?" he checked with a frown, and stretched his hand a little further towards her.

Polly realized her arms were still hanging by her sides. Colour whooshed into her cheeks. She hesitantly put her hand in his, trying to ignore the way her heart thumped at the feel of his skin. He folded his fingers around hers and steadied her as she started to climb towards the boat. His grip was strong and safe.

Now is not the time for daydreaming, Polly instructed herself, suddenly feeling embarrassed. *Now is the time for concentrating. You don't want to tip the whole. . .*

"Ahhh!"

The last rock slid away from her foot and landed with a splash in the sea. Polly lost her balance completely. With her arms flailing, she lunged into the boat head first, tackling the boy around the knees and hitting the deck with a crunch. She watched, frozen with horror at what she had done, as he staggered backwards, caught his foot against a rope and started to fall towards the water.

"Oh . . . no!"

Polly scrambled to her feet and threw her arms around him, trying to pull him back. Her sudden movement made the boat rock worse than ever.

And then the whole world tipped sideways and she crashed into the dark and freezing water, bottom first, with her arms still wrapped around her rescuer's waist.

FIVE

Polly fought her way to the surface, coughing and spluttering. Falling into the sea hadn't featured in her little daydream, and with good reason. The water was *freezing*, and the waves buffeted her mercilessly from side to side.

She kicked hard, feeling clumsy in her heavy shoes, with her sodden fringe in her eyes and her heart racing like a frightened rabbit. Where was everything? The boat? The rocks? And what about the boy – she blushed miserably – the boy she'd pulled overboard?

I'll never live this down, she thought in despair. If he didn't think she was an idiot before, now he would for sure.

A big wave knocked her sideways and she

swallowed a mouthful of salt water. Her skirt was getting heavier, dragging her downwards, and when a rock loomed dangerously close to her head, she panicked and started to scream. This was all her worst nightmares coming true. Dashed against the rocks, knocked unconscious, drowned. . .

A dark head bobbed up beside her, and a hand grabbed her own.

"I've got you," he said in her ear. His breath was warm against her cold cheek. "The boat's not far. Can you make it?"

Polly felt calmer as she glimpsed the white hull of the *Arctic Angel* floating just behind her rescuer. She kicked hard, grateful for the feeling of the boy's hand. The moment they reached the boat, he heaved himself out of the water before grasping her by both hands and pulling her aboard beside him.

They lay side by side, coughing. Polly wanted to die of shame, or cold, or maybe both. Her romantic daydream had turned into a horrible disaster!

He stopped coughing and rolled on to his side with his chin propped in his hand, seawater pooling on the deck around him.

"I'm Sam," he said cheerfully, as if she hadn't tipped him into the sea and almost drowned them both.

"P . . . P . . . Polly," Polly gasped, shivering.

"Pleased to meet you, P-P-Polly."

"That was totally my fault," she moaned. "You must hate me."

"It was the rock's fault," he pointed out.

Rock or no rock, Polly still felt utterly stupid. She should have been concentrating on where she was putting her feet, not imagining what it would feel like to have this boy's arms round her.

"We need to dry off before we freeze," he said, getting to his feet.

He pulled his soaked jumper over his head and dropped it in a soggy heap on the deck. Polly felt herself going bright red at the sight of his bare brown chest, and quickly turned her head away.

The next thing she knew, he was in a dry sweatshirt and draping a warm blanket around her.

"Are you OK?" he said, resting his hands on her shoulders and looking into her eyes. "I'm sorry I don't have any clothes aboard for you, but the blanket will help."

She felt warmed by the concern in his bright hazel eyes, so close in colour to her own. "This is nothing to a British mermaid," she quipped. The feel of his hands was making her tremble more than the cold or the shock. "Those Caribbean ones would be in trouble, though."

He laughed. "I'll get the boat under control. We'll be ashore in a few minutes."

He furled the flapping sails, and Polly felt the boat throb to life beneath her as he started the outboard motor to bring them into shore.

The moment the keel of the boat bumped up against the beach, Sam jumped into the water and lifted Polly down. It was wonderful to feel the hard sandy ridges beneath her feet again. Out in the sea, the rock where she had been perched was almost completely submerged.

"Come here," he said.

To Polly's astonishment, Sam wrapped her in a hug. She froze, wondering what to do. He smelled salty and damp and delicious.

"Body warmth," he said into her hair. "We're both frozen. Unless you want hypothermia, I suggest you hug me back."

Polly was grateful for the near darkness, because her face was on fire. She'd never hugged a boy she didn't know before. He was right, of course – she had read about the importance of body warmth in dangerous situations. Even with her blanket, she was still shivering hopelessly. Obediently she wrapped her arms around him and tried not to noticed the hard muscles of his back beneath her fingers.

"That's better," he said. He pulled back a little so he could look at her face. "So, P-P-Polly. Do you live in Heartside?"

It was wonderfully weird, introducing themselves while wrapped in a full-body hug, thought Polly. She felt a giggle welling up inside her. She could get used to conversations like this.

Sam was seventeen, and a pupil at the private Langham Academy a few miles further down the coast.

"I've been there since I was thirteen," he explained into her hair. "I'm going to study political science at university if I get the grades."

"You're into politics?" said Polly in wonder. This guy just got better and better.

"Green issues, mainly. I'm working on a big project at the moment, on the plight of seals. Have you ever seen a seal in Heartside?"

Polly shook her head.

"Exactly." Sam sounded grim. "There used to be a colony of them a little further down the coast. Now they've gone. Shipping lanes, dredging, cruise ships – all these commercial marine operations are killing or displacing our natural coastal wildlife. It's a scandal happening all over Britain. I've been out photographing evidence for our local MP, who's bringing a bill before Parliament next week before we lose our seals for good. We're putting a pamphlet together to raise awareness, and organizing a protest too."

He is incredible, Polly thought, feeling dazed. *My perfect guy.*

"It's not much." He rubbed Polly's back, making her want to arch like a cat. "But I want to try and make things better."

Was he pulling her closer, or was it her imagination? Polly wanted to stay like this for ever. But there was no getting away from the fact that her clothes weren't getting any drier in Sam's embrace.

"Do you think we should make a fire?" she said reluctantly against his chest.

She felt the chill of the evening air again as he slowly let her go. "Good idea. There's some driftwood over there."

Keeping the blanket wrapped firmly round herself, Polly moved along the tideline in a dream, picking up dry pieces of wood for kindling. She'd done the same for the campfire in the secret cove only two hours earlier. It felt like a lifetime ago. All she wanted to do was snuggle back into Sam's arms. He was smart, funny, cared about things, and he was completely gorgeous. And she thought that maybe he liked her back, and felt the same connection that she did. It was too much to take in.

They built a fire close to the sweep of the rocks, shielded from prying eyes. Soon they had the driftwood spitting salty blue-green flames. The sun's final rays spilled across the sea like liquid gold, or a path to somewhere magical, far away over the horizon. Polly let the warmth wash over her. When Sam's arm came round her again, it felt like the most natural thing in the world.

"This will probably sound weird," he said apologetically, "but I feel as if I've known you for ages."

"It's my mermaid powers," she said, snuggling closer. "We do it to all the guys we push off boats."

Sam rested his head against her forehead, then took her hand and rubbed it gently with his thumb.

He's going to kiss me, she thought ecstatically. This drumming in her heart had none of the uncertainty she had felt with Liam only a few hours earlier.

Her brain skimmed from Liam to Ollie. Dismayed, she shook her head to dislodge the thought. For once, why couldn't she turn off her brain and be in the moment?

SIX

"What are you thinking?" Sam murmured, his eyes questioning.

I'm thinking of you, Polly told herself. Everything about Sam, the fire and the sunset and the beach, was utterly perfect. Even their dunk in the freezing sea had an air of romance about it. She wouldn't let herself ruin the magic.

"I was thinking," she said, gazing into his warm hazel eyes, "of doing this."

She leaned towards him and kissed him on the lips. There was a flash of delight on his face, and then he gathered her into him and kissed her back.

His hands held her face so gently, and his lips were soft and searching. She felt as though she were melting against him. He tasted of salt and the smoke of the fire, and as their kiss deepened she found herself winding her hands around his neck and pulling him closer. He tugged softly at her bottom lip with his teeth, exploring her mouth as intently as she was exploring his. Pleasure shot through her like fire. How could she ever have thought of kissing Liam? *This* was the perfect first kiss that she'd been waiting for.

"Polly!"

Polly opened her eyes, feeling a little dazed. Her name was on the wind. Someone was shouting for her. Someone that sounded like Lila.

"Kiss me again," Sam whispered, pulling her back towards him. The feeling of his mouth on hers was indescribably wonderful—

"*Polly!*"

Polly came back to reality with a jolt. It *was* Lila, and she sounded worried.

A second voice joined in. "POLLY! Where are you?"

Ollie had joined the hunt. Any moment now, he and Lila would come round the top of the rocks by the clock tower and see her with Sam.

Polly's first coherent thought was clear. *Stop them before they see us.* It was an odd thought, she knew. But she wanted Sam for herself. The spell would be broken if too many people knew about it. She knew that as surely as she knew anything. It was their moment, hers and Sam's, and nobody else's.

"I'll be right back," she promised, trailing her fingers through Sam's short dark hair. Shrugging off the blanket, she got quickly to her feet. "Don't go away."

She broke into a run up the beach, right to the top of the rocks. Then she veered right past the clock tower and down to the stretch of sand on the other side. There she stopped to catch her breath, resting her hands on her knees.

"I'm here," she gasped, raising one arm to wave as Lila and Ollie approached, hand in hand, with worried expressions on their faces. "I'm fine."'

"Polly!" Lila dropped Ollie's hand and ran up to her. "Your clothes . . . your hair! You're *drenched*. What happened to you?"

"You've been gone for ages," Ollie complained.

Polly felt a flicker of pleasure. Ollie had noticed

she was gone. But the flicker had none of the old sting about it. It was strange standing so close to him, but feeling so far away at the same time. She had never thought it could happen. Right now, all she wanted to do was distract her friends and run back into Sam's waiting arms.

"I . . . it's nothing, I was walking by the water and a big wave caught me by surprise," she lied.

"It must have been a heck of a wave," said Ollie, looking at the way her top clung damply to her skin.

"It was. I should have had a surfboard!" The joke sounded stilted, even to Polly's own ears. Would they realize she was lying to them?

Ollie started singing a surfing tune, lifting his arms and pretending to ride a wave. Lila laughed and shoved him in the ribs, making him topple backwards.

"No!" Ollie shouted, flailing around dramatically. "I'm drowning! A shark! A jellyfish! A jelly shark!"

Lila put her hands on her hips. "Strawberry flavoured? They're the most dangerous, I hear."

Ollie continued groaning, rolling around on the sand by her feet.

Lila rolled her eyes. "I suggest we ignore him," she

said. Her face grew serious again. "Where have you been, Pol? We've been looking for you for over an hour. Seriously, we thought you'd been swept out to sea."

She wasn't far wrong, Polly thought.

"You know how it can be sometimes," she said aloud, choosing her words carefully. "I was just walking, clearing my head. I lost track of time. I'm sorry you were worried, but as you can see, I'm fine. Listen, I think I need to head home, get some dry clothes. You guys go back to the party."

"Are you sure?" said Ollie, getting to his feet and dusting the sand off his jeans. "We can walk you back."

"No," Polly said, so quickly that Lila frowned in surprise. "I mean, don't miss the party on my account. It's not far and I'm pretty tired."

Lila looked back over her shoulder, towards the secret cove. Polly could just hear the beat of music above the crash of the waves. "Well, if you're sure. . ."

"I am," Polly said firmly.

Ollie raised his hands. "You're the boss. But I'm eating your marshmallows."

She wished they would hurry up and leave. She managed a smile. "Fine. Just go before someone else gets them."

Ollie groaned in pretend panic and started pulling Lila back towards the party.

"Don't get hypothermia, OK?" Lila called back. "I'll call you later!"

Polly waited until they were out of sight, jigging impatiently from foot to foot. If they saw her heading down towards the water instead of home, they might come back and ask her more questions. And she really, *really* didn't want them to do that.

Finally they were gone. Polly spun on the spot, raced back past the clock tower, jumped down into the sand on the other side – and stopped in dismay.

The boat had gone. And so had Sam.

SEVEN

Polly rubbed her eyes, willing Sam to be there. But there was nothing. Just the sea washing against the rocks, and a pair of squabbling gulls that flapped away as she approached. She could hardly breathe for disappointment.

Did I dream it? she wondered wildly. The whole thing had been strangely dreamlike. The drama on the rocks, the sighting of the boat, the catastrophic rescue and the incredible kiss. She brought her fingers to her mouth. She could still feel Sam's lips on hers. How could she have kissed a dream?

The sad remains of the campfire they had built, its flames doused by the creeping tide, proved that it had been real. But how could Sam have vanished without a word, without even a hint that he had been there with her? She thought they had both felt their amazing connection. But as usual, she was wrong.

Tears blurred Polly's eyes as she scuffed her toe through the charred, floating driftwood by her feet. There was something tragic and poetic about the dying campfire. It was just like her love life: burning bright for one moment and extinguished the next.

Why do the men in my life all disappear? she thought in despair. First her dad, and now Sam. She didn't think she could bear it.

Polly tried to find a way of stopping herself from sinking into total gloom. *It's better this way*, she told herself as she wiped the treacherous tears from her eyes. Romance was more trouble than it was worth. Her parents had once been in love, and look what had happened to them. Relationships never worked. Why even start them?

Polly grimaced as she remembered how much she used to love the story about how her parents had met. She could see her mum's face creased into a sunny smile as she went into all the details around the scrubbed kitchen table with its view of San Francisco

Bay. How she had just graduated from university in Britain and was travelling across the States looking for adventure; how she had literally bumped into Polly's dad while running for one of the cute little trams that wheezed up and down San Francisco's hills; how he had wowed her with his unconventional approach to life; and how they had married almost at once and settled in that beautiful city with its red bridge, its strange foggy weather, and the unpredictability of the ground under your feet, which would shiver every now and again like a dog shaking water off its fur.

"Do you know," her mum would say, laughing as her dad laid his blond head on the kitchen table pretending to cover his ears, "when we first met, your dad hadn't changed his clothes in *three weeks*? I thought he was a vagrant!"

"It was *research*!" her dad used to protest in his warm American voice, peeking a little through his fingers with his head still on the table. "You can't write a thesis about living off the urban landscape with only your wits keeping you from total destitution without experiencing it for real."

"You certainly did that," Polly's mum had replied, ruffling his hair affectionately. "So did everyone else on that tram. The smell of you!"

"You didn't think I smelled so bad at the time," Polly's dad reminded her. And they had smiled at each other in a way that made Polly feel warm inside.

Her parents had been magical together once, before their differences broke them apart and the world came tumbling down around Polly's ears. Suddenly it was all screaming and shouting, slamming doors and packing suitcases. Her dad leaving, and her mother crying. And then San Francisco had fallen away beneath the wings of the aeroplane, bringing Polly's mother home, and Polly to a cold, crowded place full of strange customs, tiny roads and the horrible reality of wearing the exact same school uniform day after day instead of the brightly coloured tunics, zebra-print leggings and sneakers with glittery laces she had worn in the past. Even now, six years on, she felt as if she had left more than just her heart back in the States. She had left her identity there as well.

It's best to leave Sam as just one perfect memory, she consoled herself. *Not even I can ruin a memory.*

She turned away from the sea and trudged up the beach. Suddenly the thought of a warm shower, cosy slippers and her fluffy onesie consumed her. She would use her favourite organic shampoo, and break open the new pot of body cream she had been saving since her birthday. She would throw away the skirt which had brought her so much trouble today, and fix up the perfect outfit for tomorrow. She would forget about all the plans and hopes she'd had, of walking on the beach with Sam and holding his hand and maybe even taking him to Kissing Island by the light of a full moon, where they would kiss and dream and talk about the stars.

Don't think about what could have been, she ordered herself fiercely. *There's no point. Just walk faster*. Her feet were like blocks of ice.

As she turned into her road, a figure detached itself from the pillar by her driveway.

"Hi," said Eve. "I was waiting for you."

Eve was the last person Polly wanted to see. She smoothed down her damp hair as best she could and folded her arms like a barrier between them.

Eve's face was pale in the streetlight. She jammed

her hands deep into her coat pockets. "I wanted to talk about earlier. When you saw me, you know. . ."

"Making out with your best friend's boyfriend?" Polly enquired.

Eve fiddled with a lock of auburn hair. "Max, yes."

"And you're here so I can congratulate you?" Polly was in no mood for making Eve feel better about what she'd done.

"Of course not!" said Eve. "I just wanted a private word about it."

"You have one minute," Polly said. Her teeth were starting to chatter again. She had to get inside before hypothermia became a genuine concern.

"I just wanted to know. . ." Eve began. She shifted her weight to her other foot and fiddled with her hair again. "What will it take to keep you quiet about me and Max?"

"What?"

"We don't want this getting back to Rhi," Eve said.

The way she said "we" made Polly realize something. "That wasn't the first time, was it?" she said incredulously.

Eve lifted her chin. "We've been seeing each other

for a couple of weeks. Since Valentine's Day, actually. What Rhi doesn't know can't hurt her."

Eve was unbelievable, thought Polly. How could she behave so badly towards her best friend? She squirmed a little as she thought of the fantasies she'd had about Ollie. But the difference was, she would never act on them.

"So?" said Eve impatiently. "What do you want?"

Eve wouldn't hesitate to use this kind of information for evil purposes. She assumed Polly would do the same. Eve didn't know her at all.

"I would love the world to see you for the nasty person that you really are," Polly answered coolly. "I might start dropping hints in the corridor after half-term."

Eve went paler. "You wouldn't. Would you? Rhi would totally kill us both."

Rhi was more likely to shatter with misery, Polly thought. Eve Somerstown understood nothing about broken hearts. She wanted Eve to leave.

"All I want is for you to leave Lila alone," she said, feeling bone weary. "Stop all your tricks and wind-ups. Enough is enough, Eve."

Eve scuffed the ground. "And if I do, you'll stay quiet? No hints, nothing?"

"Go home," Polly said coldly, and headed up her driveway without looking back. She could feel Eve's eyes watching her.

"Fine," Eve called after her. "But if Rhi finds out, let's just say I'll know who to blame."

Eve's footsteps echoed away down the road. But Polly wasn't listening any more. Her eyes were fixed on someone else waiting in the driveway, his car parked up against the laurel bushes by the front door. She couldn't process what she was seeing.

"Dad?" she said in disbelief.

"Hey, Polly Dolly," said her father with a broad smile. He lifted his arms hopefully towards her. "Give your old dad a hug?"

Polly's feet wouldn't move. "What are you doing here?" she managed.

When it was clear Polly wasn't going to run into his arms, her father tucked his hands into his pockets and cleared his throat. "Your mother asked the same question. She's locked me out of the house." He nodded at the tightly shut front door.

Polly started trembling. The shock of seeing him standing there, like he'd done nothing, like everything was normal. . . It was too much. She hadn't seen or heard from him in months, not since the last argument her parents had had in this exact same driveway, complete with smashing dishes and a call to the police from concerned neighbours.

"Why didn't you tell me you were coming?"

She knew the question sounded sharp. She couldn't help it.

"I tried." Her father pulled a face and looked at the front door again. "Your mom must have intercepted all my messages." He held out his arms again. "I didn't come to see her, though. I came to see you."

Polly wanted to fall into his arms and cry all over his shirt. Her feet still wouldn't move.

The front door opened.

"Get inside, Polly," said her mother, in the hard voice Polly knew so well. "Your father is leaving."

"I have a right to see my daughter, Ginny," protested her dad. "You can't keep me away from her."

Polly's mother glared at him. "Watch me, Alex! Polly? Inside."

Polly looked from her mother's furious face to her father's crumpled, disappointed one. Tears gleamed in his eyes.

"Inside *now*," her mother repeated in a voice of iron.

Polly moved, ghostlike, towards the door.

"Call me," she said quietly as she passed her dad, so only he could hear.

EIGHT

Polly sat in the middle of a pile of fabric and groaned. She didn't know where to start. One minute it was like she had too many clothes, and the next, too few.

She picked up a pair of silk trousers in a purple floral pattern, turning them towards the light.

Can I wear them to lunch with Dad today? she wondered. *Or are they too crazy?*

She had found the trousers a month ago in a charity shop, and loved the fabric at once. They had fitted perfectly around her waist, but as Polly was only five feet two inches tall, the bottoms had puddled around her feet. With a couple of snips and some careful hemming, she had turned them into a really cool pair of ankle-grazing trousers that turned people's heads whenever she wore them.

As she folded the trousers carefully down the middle, lining up the seams, she noticed something that made her heart sink. The left leg was shorter than the right by a few millimetres. She checked again. There was no doubt about it.

She put the trousers down, feeling sick. She'd worked so hard on them. How could she have made such a stupid mistake?

She swallowed and looked around her room. Everything was a mess. She had to get it straight before she did anything else. How could she find what she wanted to wear when she could hardly see the floor?

Feeling flustered, she straightened everything as neatly as she could. The floral trousers were folded. Shirts went back in the wardrobe. When everything was exactly as it should be, Polly returned to her most pressing concern.

What was she going to wear for her dad?

He had called last night, on her mobile. Polly hadn't said much, aware of her mother moving around outside her bedroom.

"It's a great place, you'll love it," her dad told her about the restaurant where he wanted to take her for lunch. "It's totally vegan. Everything is sourced locally. Their oat-cookie ice cream made from coconut milk is incredible."

There was a knock on Polly's door.

"Can I come in?"

Polly had almost leaped out of her skin. Her mum would *flip* if she knew who she was talking to. "Got to go, Dad," she said, her heart hammering against her ribs. "See you there at twelve-thirty tomorrow."

"Bye, Polly Dol—"

She had slammed her phone shut, cutting him off, just as her mother had opened her bedroom door. It had been a close call in more ways than one.

Wiping her forehead and straightening her jumpers once more, she checked the time. Nearly twelve o'clock. If she didn't hurry up, she'd be late. Why was this so *hard*?

Her phone rang. For one mad moment, Polly wondered if it could be Sam. He might have found her number somehow, and be calling her. . . Just as quickly, she pushed the thought away. He hadn't been interested enough to stick around last night. And how would he have tracked down her mobile number anyway?

The caller display said: *Lila*.

Polly ignored it. Lila had called three times already this morning, but she hadn't felt up to a conversation. She was too stressed about lunch, and Sam, and her confusing feelings for Ollie. She was so sick of it all.

Her mother knocked.

"Come in," Polly said wearily.

"You OK in here?" her mother asked. "You've been a while."

Polly shrugged. What could she say? *I'm meeting your worst enemy for lunch in half an hour?*

"I'm getting ready to go out with Lila," she lied.

Her mum studied the pristine room, and Polly still in her PJs. "You don't look ready to me."

"It takes a while," she said vaguely. "You know. Deciding what to wear."

Her mother hesitated at the door. Polly could tell she wanted to chat. She snatched another glimpse at the time. She was running seriously late now.

"I don't want you seeing your father," said her mother abruptly. "I know him and I know he's up to something. Has he contacted you?"

Polly had been expecting it, but it still felt like a blow. "You sent him away last night," she said, careful not to answer her mother's question. "How could he have contacted me?"

Her mother put her hands on her hips. "That *man*," she said furiously. "Who does he think he is, turning up unannounced? I don't want him unsettling you, Polly. Did you know he's buying a *farm*?"

This was real news to Polly, so it was easy to look surprised. "Where?"

"His beloved California, of course. He wants to go completely off-grid. No computer, no phone, growing his own food." She shook her head in contempt. "Typical. No idea of how to live in the real world. He really has lost his mind this time."

Polly thought it sounded like a brilliant idea, but she stayed silent, determined not to take sides.

Her phone rang again. She froze.

"It's Lila," said her mum, glancing at the phone lying on Polly's bed.

Thank goodness, Polly thought. *It would have been a nightmare if it had been Dad.*

"We need to work out last-minute details," she lied, reaching out her hand as if to answer the phone. "See you later, Mum."

Her mother left the room, still muttering about Polly's dad.

Polly let the phone shrill on in her hand until it fell silent. Suddenly she felt bad about meeting her father. She should call and cancel. It wasn't fair on her mum, keeping secrets. It was getting late anyway.

She started dialling the number that he had left – the farmhouse where he was camping. But she faltered on the last digit. He would be so disappointed. If she was honest, she would be disappointed too.

Before she had finished dialling, she hung up. Her nerves were jangling like bells, and her heart had started racing the way it always did when she was super-anxious.

Focus, she told herself.

Returning to her wardrobe, she started pulling out clothes again. There was a bad seam here, and a button hanging off there. Nothing was right. The only thing she liked was the dress she was working on at the moment, but the hem still needed doing. She couldn't fix it in five minutes.

At last she pulled on an old blue tea dress with tiny white polka dots and finished it off with a wide belt. Slipping on her brogues, she adjusted the shoelaces until the ends matched perfectly. Then she brushed her hair exactly one hundred times, fifty each side, and fixed in a pair of hair clips. Another five minutes passed as she fiddled with the clips until they matched, and tried to calm her breathing.

People deceived each other all the time. She could do this.

NINE

Polly could hardly breathe, she was laughing so much.

"And then you won't believe what happened next, Polly-Dolly," her father said, leaning across the table. "The bull started charging and bellowing something. I won't translate, but the gist was, 'Hey, two-legs, put your hands away and get outta ma field'."

"And you're actually going to *buy* him?" Polly choked. "He'll eat you for lunch, Dad!"

"He and I will get along just fine," said her dad. "As long as I never mistake him for a cow again." His hazel eyes twinkled at her, his fingers fiddling with the remains of the most delicious granary bread Polly had ever eaten.

Polly was full, and happy, and relaxed. Her dad was really *talking* to her, like she couldn't remember him talking to her before – as if her opinion really mattered, as if he was listening to every word she said in return. He was treating her like an adult, not a child, she realized. It was an amazing feeling.

He had been right about the restaurant. Although she had arrived late and flustered, it wasn't long before she forgot her nerves and gorged herself on an amazing salad of roasted beetroot and tart apple with cashew cream, followed by aubergine curry and then the famous coconut milk oat-cookie ice cream topped with fresh blackberries. They had drunk fresh-squeezed carrot-apple juice and now sat with two mugs of steaming peppermint tea, picking over the details of their lives. In some ways it was as if the last six years had never happened – and in other ways, it was as if she had gone from nine to fifteen years old in a single second. She had never realized how alike they were, in the things that mattered to them and the things that made them laugh.

"And the farm is north of San Francisco?" she said eagerly. "Do you have pictures? Do you have a view?"

He pressed his hands to his heart. "The view is like heaven. Rolling vineyards, and pine groves, and a stream that winds through the valley like a glinting steel ribbon. You are going to *love* it."

"Do you have pictures?"

Her dad shook his head. "Who needs pictures when you have this?" And he tapped his forehead.

"Insanity?" Polly laughed.

He grinned back. "Imagination. The buildings are in a bad state, but I'm going to rebuild using local materials. I'm going completely carbon-neutral. I'll have a turbine, and a heat pump sunk into the ground. We'll have solar panels everywhere. And I'm going to open a store in the outbuildings. We'll focus on sustainability, recycling, natural products. I could definitely sell some of your clothes." He looked admiringly at her outfit. "Upcycled, yes? Great buttons."

Polly felt heady with delight. "They're shells," she said shyly, fiddling with the tiny buttons down the front of her dress. "I collected them on the beach last year."

"I can see that." He smiled, shaking his head. "That's real creativity, Polly. Using the natural world without exploiting it. They go crazy for that stuff in California."

"Do you really think you could sell my clothes?" Polly said, feeling excited. "I have so many ideas, Dad. It drives me crazy, the things people get rid of. Beautiful clothes that just need a little love to turn them around and put them out in the world again."

Her father pointed a triumphant finger at her. "That is a great slogan. 'Turned around with love'."

Polly's mind was filled to bursting with ideas about what she might make for her dad to sell. Buttons were easy, and they transformed the plainest of outfits. She should do a special line of natural buttons – shells, driftwood, seed heads. . . She could picture the store already: an old barn in the California hills, scented with freshly sawn wood and filled with unique products. And they would definitely need a website. She could help design that too.

Her dad reached across the table and took her arm, pulling her out of her dreams.

"I have something I want to ask you," he said.

Polly wondered why her father looked so serious. "Ask me whatever you want, Dad," she said warmly.

He ran a hand through his thick sun-bleached hair. He looked nervous.

"Would you consider moving back to California?" he blurted. "To live with me again?"

Polly stared at him.

"You don't have to decide right away," her dad went on quickly. "It's a big decision. Leaving all your friends, and your school, and your mother. But we could do so much together back home, Polly. You could help me with the farm, and with setting up the store. And I've missed so much of you growing up. I'd like to be there for whatever's left."

Polly didn't know what to think. She would see California again! But there was a big difference between visiting and staying there for good. Could she uproot everything and go back to the States? Maybe it was the answer. She had loved her life in San Francisco, and she missed her father terribly. And it wasn't as if things were all that great here. There were her confusing feelings for Ollie, and the way her heart was breaking over Sam. Her mother wasn't easy to live with, and sometimes, when they argued, Polly could understand why her dad had left. What was keeping her in Heartside Bay?

"Are you serious?" she asked weakly.

"I've never been more serious about anything in my life," said her father. He signalled for the bill. "Will you think about it?"

Polly nodded. "Definitely."

His face blazed with delight. "Really? It would mean so much. We could make a really great life together out there. We make a good team, don't we?"

He lifted his fist to bump knuckles, which Polly returned. There was no denying it. She and her dad did make a good team.

As her dad paid the bill, Polly imagined how her life could be back in California. There would be colour and sunshine, creativity and cute high-school boys to take her mind off the ones she would leave behind. On the face of it, it was a no-brainer. She should definitely go.

Her phone started buzzing. Her head still full of California sunshine and organic fashion, Polly lifted her phone from her bag and looked at the screen.

Mum

Her blood turned to ice, congealing in her veins. She sat there, frozen, until the phone stopped buzzing. Then she noticed she had a text from Lila.

Came over to see u but u werent there.
Think I landed u in it with ur mum.
Really sorry.xx

Polly felt like a trapped animal. Her mum knew she wasn't with Lila. She was in so much trouble.

Another text popped up on the screen.

I WANT YOU HOME AT ONCE.
THIS HAD BETTER BE GOOD.
MUM

"You OK, Polly-Dolly?" asked her dad as he pocketed his wallet.

Polly shook her head. "Mum knows we're together," she said, swallowing hard.

Her dad looked nervous but defiant. "You're my daughter. We can see each other if we want. You mother can't stop us."

Polly groped for the happiness she had been feeling for the past two hours, but it had gone. Sensing her mood, her father quietly helped her put on her coat. They left the restaurant in silence.

Polly stared out of her dad's rental car window, but she didn't see the houses, or the sea, or the gulls, or any of the things she normally loved about Heartside Bay. She picked at the buttons on her dress, finding a crack in one of the shell buttons with the side of her finger. She took hold and tugged until it came away in her hand, then wound down the window so she could throw it away.

The shouting started as soon as her dad had parked the car.

"This is typical of you," her mum hissed, jabbing her dad hard in the chest with a stiff finger. "Irresponsible. *Underhand*. You have no idea what Polly went through when you left. And you think you can just swan in and out of her life whenever you feel like it—"

Polly kept her head bowed. *It'll be over soon*, she thought.

Her mother rounded on her. "I thought more of you

than this, Polly," she said. The disappointment in her voice made Polly want to curl up and disappear. "I told you I didn't want you seeing your father. And what do you do? You lie to me. You're as bad as he is!"

"Don't blame Polly for this," her father shouted, his cheeks mottled red with anger.

"Don't worry," her mother shouted back. "I'm very clear exactly who to blame here. Go to your room, Polly."

Her father caught Polly by the wrist as she moved slowly past him. "I'm in the UK for a few days on business," he said, trying to smile at her. "We'll catch up again before I leave, OK?"

"You can't just 'catch up' on six years of her life—" Polly's mum raved.

Polly trudged up the stairs, her dress flapping open where she had ripped away the button. Locking her bedroom door behind her, she flopped on to the bed and stared at the ceiling. She could still hear them tearing each other's throats out downstairs. All her unhappy memories of California came flooding back. Could she really go back to the place where everything had turned sour?

She turned up her music full blast to drown out their voices. Then she took off her dress and stuffed it to the back of her cupboard. Slipping into her favourite pyjamas, she picked up her current sewing project and tried to focus on her needle. When she pricked her finger and marked the fabric with a splash of blood, she threw the whole thing in the bin. Then she buried her head in her pillow and cried.

TEN

Polly slept in on Sunday morning. She felt completely exhausted after the dramas of the day before. If she stayed where she was, she reasoned, then she wouldn't have to face any of it.

After her dad had gone, her mum had given her a strict lecture.

"You can't trust him, love," she said, laying a hand on Polly's stiff shoulder. "I couldn't bear it if he broke your heart again."

Polly wondered how many times a heart could break before it stayed broken for ever. She pictured it in her chest, covered in a maze of fracture lines that didn't quite match.

Her mum had been angry with her yesterday, but

not angry enough to confiscate her phone. She rolled over and sleepily poked around on her bedside table until she found it. Yawning and squinting in the bright light pouring through her thin curtains, she looked at her phone and saw she had two texts.

Suns shining so were going sailing.
Leaving the harbour at 2. Dont be late.
E

The text read more like an order than an invitation. It was as if Eve couldn't imagine anyone saying no. Her family owned a luxurious yacht. *Typical*, thought Polly. Given how they had parted on Friday, Polly was surprised she was on the invite list at all.

She checked who Eve had sent the message to. Lila, Ollie, Rhi, Max, a couple of others.

The next text was from Lila.

U OK?
U annoyed with me?
U doing Eves boat thing?
L xx

Polly felt guilty. Lila hadn't known about Polly's secret plan to meet her dad. It wasn't her fault that she'd alerted Polly's mum to what was really going on. Polly had been ignoring her calls because it was just too stressful, talking to Lila and hiding her feelings for Ollie at the same time. She couldn't let Lila think it was because she was angry with her.

"Hey," she said when Lila picked up on the second ring.

"Polly!" Lila almost shouted in relief. "What's going on? I'm really sorry, you know, about yesterday. Who were you meeting? Your mum was really mad. Did I get you in trouble? I'm really sorry if—"

"It's fine, I'm not mad with you," Polly interrupted Lila's frantic stream of apologies. *Normal voice*, she told herself. It was hard, but she did her best. "I'm sorry I didn't call yesterday. It was kind of difficult."

She told Lila about her dad and the restaurant, careful not to mention the idea of moving out to California. She still wasn't sure how she felt about that. Lila listened without interrupting.

"That's bad," Lila said at last. "Is there anything I can do?"

Polly's eyes pricked with tears. She didn't deserve someone like Lila as a friend.

"You can take my mind off it," she said, feeling grateful. "Are you doing Eve's boat trip?"

"I don't know," said Lila uncertainly. "Eve will probably try and push me off the boat in deep water. Why has she invited me, do you think? Everyone knows she hates my guts."

Polly thought about the conversation she'd had with Eve on Friday night. "Maybe she's finally decided to make peace," she said.

Lila snorted. "And maybe the sun's started setting in the east! Whose boat is it, anyway?"

"Her dad's, I guess. He keeps it at the old yacht club to the west of the pier."

"Do you think we should go?" Lila still sounded unconvinced.

Polly got out of bed and pulled back her curtains. The sky was a brilliant cloudless blue, a rare day of pure sunshine, and unusually warm for the time of year. Maybe Eve really was living up to her half of the bargain they'd made about Max.

"The weather's gorgeous," she said, dropping the

curtain again. "And it's an afternoon and evening on a glamorous yacht. I don't think we can refuse."

"It's a tough choice," said Lila. Polly could hear her grinning on the other end of the phone. "But I guess we all have to suffer for our fun. If Ollie and I come, you have to promise you'll watch my back, OK? I don't want to get tied in chains and thrown overboard with the anchor. To be honest, you've gone so quiet over the past couple of days I wondered if Eve had assassinated you already."

Polly tried not to wince at Lila's casual mention of Ollie. "I'm really sorry you got caught up in my family nightmares. But it's not the only thing I've had going on." She gathered her courage. "I met this boy."

Lila squealed. "What? Where? When? Did you kiss him?"

Polly was remembering the warmth of Sam's lips on hers. "What?" she said, trying to concentrate on the conversation. "Oh. Yes, I did. It was on the beach on Friday when you were looking for me."

"I can't believe you kissed a boy and didn't tell me," Lila complained. "Was it someone from school? Was it that Liam guy you were with by the fire?"

"No," said Polly. "He's called Sam, and he has a boat. But don't get too excited. I lost him five minutes later."

"How can you lose a guy?" Lila sounded confused.

"I don't know," Polly said. She still hadn't figured that out. People generally didn't vanish the way Sam had. "But I did. So I've had that on my mind too."

"No wonder you've been so preoccupied," said Lila. "I'm sorry it went wrong for you, Polly. But how romantic! Meeting a boy and kissing him straight away. Was he a good kisser?"

"Amazing," said Polly, flushing at the memory again. "I mean, I don't have anything to compare it to, but . . . it felt really great."

Lila laughed. "He was, then."

Polly wanted to tell Lila so much more. About California, and how she'd seen Eve and Max kissing, and all the worries and anxieties that were eating her up all the time. But she couldn't.

"So you'll definitely be at the harbour at two?" Lila checked. "There's no way Ollie and I are going if you're not coming too."

Polly left Lila with the promise that she would

be there at two. Then, after a long shower, she straightened her room and went downstairs, hunting for something to eat. Her mum was at work, showing buyers around houses, and had left a note on the kitchen table saying she wouldn't be back until five. Weekends were always busy for estate agents, who often had to fit around other people's normal working weeks.

And don't answer the phone if your father calls again, her mother had added to the message. *I want him to leave you alone.*

Polly finished a tub of hummus, two pittas, a carrot and an apple, then went back upstairs again. What was she going to wear?

Everything she took from her wardrobe seemed wrong like it had the day before, ill-fitting or badly made. She discarded the uneven trousers at once, and didn't even look at the dress with the missing shell button. She took the dress she had been hemming out of the bin and studied it carefully.

She had found it in a car boot sale, its bright yellow flowers and splashes of blue catching her eye at once. It was stupid to throw it out before she'd had a chance to wear it. Maybe she could sponge the stain out. The hem wouldn't take long.

After ten minutes at the sink, the bloodstain had gone. Polly threaded a needle and stitched the hem in properly. Then she ironed it and prepared to put it on.

It was a seventies style, with a flared skirt and no sleeves. She twirled in front of the mirror, trying to decide if the hem was straight. When she stood front-on, it looked OK. But was it riding up at the back?

Calm, Polly told herself. She checked her watch. She still had an hour before the boat left. She stood with her back to the mirror, checking the hem. The yellow and blue pattern blurred in front of her eyes. It was definitely uneven.

Wriggling out of the dress, she attempted the hem again, and reironed the result. Again she positioned herself in front of the mirror. Was it shorter on one side now, or was it her imagination?

She slammed her wardrobe door. The mirror wasn't helping. She still had to do her make-up and jewellery.

Settling on a pair of white-and-yellow daisy earrings, she slipped her feet into a pair of black flats she had customized over the summer with a row of silver beads across the toe, and opened the wardrobe door again to study the result, resting her hands on her hips and turning in a slow circle with her eyes on the mirror.

It's all wrong, she thought in despair.

Ten more minutes passed as she took off the dress and hunted for something else. The clock on her bedroom wall now said one-thirty. She started to panic. She couldn't be late. The boat would leave without her.

You're worrying too much, she told herself. *The dress looked good. You'll be fine.*

Wearing the yellow and blue dress again, make-up done and her hair swishing around her face, she let herself out of the house. But halfway down the road, a voice started up in her head. The outfit was wrong. She couldn't do this.

She turned back. Ran home. Rushed through the front door and up the stairs. She stared hard at her reflection. A white, pinched face with anxious hazel eyes looked back at her.

You are unique, Polly Nelson, she thought, willing herself to believe it. *Be proud of who you are.*

This time she made it almost to the end of the road

before she could feel that nagging little voice again. She looked awful. Almost in tears, Polly started back towards her house. She forced herself to stop on the pavement and breathe. Her legs were trembling with nerves. Her heart was racing.

What's more important? she asked herself. *Your stupid outfit or missing that boat?*

She checked her watch and groaned. She had exactly seven minutes before she got left behind. Somehow, she found the strength to start running down the hill towards the harbour.

The sun gleamed on the water. Boats were sailing away from the dock, their sails full and billowing. Memories of Sam pierced her like arrows. She had a stitch in her side, and she stopped for a moment to catch her breath.

Great look, Polly, she told herself wryly. *Red-faced and sweating.*

She could hear someone shouting her name.

"Polly!" Rhi was waving her arms madly from the prow of a white boat that was starting to move, her cloud of dark hair pulled back from her head. *"RUN!"*

Panicking for real now, Polly put on a burst of

speed. As she reached the edge of the water, she stared with wide fearful eyes at the widening gap between the boat and the jetty, the calls and shouts from her friends. . .

She jumped.

ELEVEN

Water glinted under her feet. Music was pumping through the air, and she could hear the insistent chatter of a party. Polly just had time to remember what had happened the last time she had tried to jump aboard a boat when a pair of strong arms caught her round the waist.

"Welcome aboard, Oh Incredible Flying Girl," Ollie shouted over the music, grinning down at her. "Better late than never."

Polly's whole body went rigid. Ollie was wearing a tight blue hoodie that emphasized his strong chest and brought out the colour in his eyes. She could feel every muscle in his back as she held him, and the warmth of his palms as they pressed against her. Blood roared in her ears. She knew she should let go, but she didn't seem able to. For what felt like an age, she couldn't tear her eyes or her arms away.

"No need to smother me, thanks," Ollie added, his arms still holding her up off the deck.

Dimly Polly sensed Eve lounging at the side of the boat in a long green dress and jewelled sandals, watching them as intently as a cat might watch a mouse. With a lurch of horror, Polly realized she had let her guard down. Every dream she had ever had about Ollie – every heartbeat felt, every tear shed and every swell of emotion experienced – was written all over her face. And now Eve knew.

She pushed at Ollie's arms, her face flaming scarlet. "You can put me down now," she muttered. "I'm not a football."

There was a flash of something in his eyes that reminded Polly of the hurt she'd seen when she'd compared his brain to a marshmallow.

"Whatever," he said, putting her down abruptly on the shining wooden boards. "Nice curtain, by the way," he added, sweeping his eyes over her dress. "Very you. Is the rest of you double-glazed?"

Polly felt winded with hurt. "You probably can't even spell that," she managed. "How does it feel to have nothing between your ears but a gentle breeze?"

She wrenched herself away from his hands, which were still on her shoulders. As she did so, she heard the telltale sound of ripping fabric. Her collar hung at an awkward angle down the front of her dress. Ollie had torn it.

She ran blindly for the cabin, her hand pressed against the ruined fabric. She was aware of people parting, letting her through. All she wanted was to escape.

The cabin was dark and quiet. Several rooms led off from the long, low sitting area. Polly chose the one furthest from the deck and slammed the door behind her.

Breathe, she told herself hysterically. *Don't let this get to you.*

She was in a bedroom which seemed much too large for a boat. Pictures of yachts in full sail hung on the walls, and a jumble of clothes lay haphazardly on the polished wooden floor. She couldn't exactly help herself to the clothes lying around the room, not without asking. From the style and size, they were clearly Eve's. Polly rifled desperately through the drawers beside the bed instead. She needed a needle and thread.

I hate this dress, she thought savagely, snatching up a packet of needles and a spool of white cotton. *I wish I'd never worn it.* But she had, and she was stuck with it, and there was nothing for it but to mend the problem.

Her fingers were shaking so much that it took five attempts to thread the needle. The feeling of the sharp steel point between her fingers calmed her and focused her mind. She had to pretend Ollie had never said those horrible things to her. If only she could rewind the last five minutes!

Setting the needle down, she wriggled out of the dress and studied the damage. The collar had come away from the seam around the neck, and the fabric on the collar itself had ripped.

Polly steadied her breathing and unpicked the whole collar. When it came away from the dress, she started to slip-stitch the seams back together. In five minutes, it was a collarless dress. She held it up and examined her stitches. Given her state of mind, they were surprisingly neat.

She put the dress back on and smoothed out the skirt. Then she checked herself in the long mirror set inside one of the cupboards.

Better, she thought, feeling calmer. *Much better.* She sat down, fiddling with the fabric over her knees, trying to find the courage to leave her safe haven.

The door swung open. Eve's eyes widened at the sight of Polly on her bed.

"What the hell are you doing in my room?" she demanded, recovering.

Polly leaped up, frantically preparing excuses. How much had Eve worked out about her feelings for Ollie? Had she come across as completely crazy out there on the deck, running off the way she had?

Polly saw Max scurrying back down the corridor behind Eve, ducking his head to avoid Polly's gaze. Everything became clear. *Attack is the best form of defence*, she thought, and instantly felt calmer.

"Did I spoil your private time with your best friend's boyfriend?" she said. "Sorry about that."

Eve folded her arms. "Look who's talking," she

drawled. "That was very romantic out there on the deck, wasn't it? Don't deny it. I saw the way you looked at Ollie. Not so high and mighty after all, are you?"

"That's ridiculous," Polly bluffed. She tried to stop her voice from trembling. "You and Max are a fact, Eve. How long are you going to keep your nasty little secret?"

Eve's eyes darted from side to side, but she stayed where she was.

"We have a deal," she said.

"And our deal only lasts as long as my patience." Polly took a step forward. "If you breathe a word of your lies about me and Ollie, I will tell Rhi about Max."

Polly caught sight of Rhi's dark head appearing round the bedroom door as the last words slipped out. She gasped, putting her hand to her mouth, wishing she could push the words back in again.

Putting her arm around Eve's shoulders, Rhi smiled, intrigued by the silence that had suddenly descended.

"Tell Rhi what about Max?" she said with a laugh.

TWELVE

Polly's tongue felt as if it was stuck to the roof of her mouth. She stared at Rhi, trying to work out exactly how much Rhi had heard. She would die if she was the one to bring Rhi's illusions crashing down.

"Hey, Rhi." Eve flipped her hair back over her shoulders and leaned against the cupboards. "What are you doing down here?"

"I got a bit lost looking for Max," Rhi confessed. "This boat is huge, Eve. Is your dad planning to sail round the world one day?"

"He's talked about it," said Eve casually. "But he's always working, so I'll believe that when I see it."

How could Eve be so cool? Polly thought in

amazement. She was acting like nothing was wrong at all.

"You're really lucky," said Rhi. She ran a finger wistfully down the dark wooden panelling. "The biggest boat I'll ever have is the one in our bathtub."

Eve pinched Rhi's cheek. "Poor little baby," she said with a lopsided smile. "Hey, maybe we should make a plan for Dad's boat this summer. We could sail to France, maybe, or Spain. . ."

"The Caribbean!" Rhi suggested, her eyes shining at the prospect.

"Now *that's* what I would call a holiday," Eve agreed.

Polly could hardly watch. Eve was so hypocritical.

"Anyway,' Rhi said, smiling, "what were you saying about Max? Have you seen him? I thought I spotted him coming this way."

"No, sorry," Eve said blandly. She raised her eyebrows at Polly.

She's daring me to break the news, Polly thought. *I won't give her that satisfaction.*

"He was in the corridor behind you about five minutes ago," Polly fudged. It wasn't the whole story, but it would have to do.

Rhi rolled her eyes. "Idiot," she said fondly. "I said I was going to be at the front of the boat." She frowned, looking from Polly to Eve and back again. "What *were* you saying about Max just then?"

Eve looked at Polly steadily. *You tell her about me and Max, and I tell Lila about you and Ollie*, her eyes seemed to say.

Polly didn't want to be part of what was coming. It was up to Eve to tell Rhi the truth.

"Nothing, Rhi," she said, backing out of the bedroom door. "I should go. I think I can hear Lila. See you later."

She broke into a little jog down the corridor, keen to get out into the fresh air. The atmosphere inside the boat was stifling.

I'm so over stupid teenage boys, she thought, elbowing her way through a couple of guys play-fighting near the ship's wheel. If Max was anything to go by, they were completely untrustworthy. Sam had seemed great, but then he had vanished without a word. And she was still hurting over Ollie's jibe about her dress.

The boat was already some distance from the

harbour. Pushing through the dancing, laughing crowd on the main deck, Polly found a quiet place beside the rails and watched the crescent shape of Heartside Bay receding from view. As the white-crested waves dashed themselves against the hull beneath her feet, she lost herself in the memory of Sam: her dramatic rescue, his little boat, their amazing kiss. The sea was calming to watch. She fiddled with her new collarless neckline and looked into the depths, wondering if she might see an elusive seal.

Hearing voices, she looked up. Lila and Ollie were walking towards her, arm in arm and looking into each other's eyes. Panicking, Polly stepped backwards, almost stumbling over a coil of rope on the deck. Had they seen her? She couldn't face Ollie yet. She wasn't sure she could ever face him again.

How was it possible to hate someone and love them at the same time?

Her heart skipped as she walked swiftly out of their line of sight, diving into the crowd on the main deck again. She wished she could relax, but she couldn't.

"Get off me, you creep!"

Polly pressed herself back against the rails as Laura

Whiting, one of Eve's cronies, stalked away from a group of Ollie's laughing football mates.

"Eve should never have invited those losers," Laura muttered at Polly as she swept past. "They're a bunch of lecherous toads."

It wasn't just the jocks who were behaving like idiots, Polly realized. It was everyone. People were losing their inhibitions, laughing too hard and pretending to trip each other up, flirting and teasing loudly, dancing and daring each other to hang over the ship's rails without holding on. All the conflict, the drama, the madness – she was not in the mood for any of it.

I should never have come, she thought.

The idea of leaving the Heartside crowd behind and moving to America with her dad had never felt more appealing. Maybe it was time to think about it more seriously. She could do so much out in the States: focus on her fashion, enjoy the quiet of her dad's organic farm, make a whole new set of friends, who weren't idiots and didn't confuse her by having gorgeous boyfriends she wasn't meant to fancy.

"There you are!"

Polly spun round in surprise. If she had been concentrating, she would have seen Lila and Ollie making their way towards her. She cursed herself for not noticing their approach. It was hard enough talking to Lila and Ollie when they were all getting along. How was she supposed to have a conversation now?

Lila was looking unusually serious. Ollie stood a little way apart, his hands in his pockets and his eyes on the deck. It was clear that he hadn't forgotten their argument either.

"Is everything OK?" Polly asked nervously.

Lila folded her arms. She looked gorgeous as usual, in a short red tunic and laced deck shoes, with large earrings that jingled against her shoulders. "I don't know," she said. "You tell me."

Polly was confused. "I don't understand."

The wind blew Lila's hair around her head in a cloud of glossy brown strands. "What's going on with you and Ollie?" she said bluntly.

Polly could feel the blood draining from her face.

"W . . . what do you mean?" she stammered.

"I saw your argument," said Lila. "Why were you so late, anyway? We waited for ages on the dock. Eve kept saying you probably wouldn't come, but you had said that you would be there at two so we kept waiting and waiting... We gave up in the end and came aboard. I went to the rails to see if I could spot you, and the next thing I know you and Ollie are shouting at each other on the deck and you disappear. What's the matter?"

Polly rubbed her temples. "I ... it's the whole thing with my dad, it's doing my head in," she lied uncomfortably. "And I just got a shock when Ollie caught me. I thought I was going to fall into the water. There's no problem. Seriously."

"But why are you avoiding me?" Tears trembled in the corners of Lila's blue eyes. "I saw you walking away earlier, like you couldn't wait to be out of my sight. I thought we were friends. I'd die without you at Heartside."

Polly felt even worse than she had been feeling already. None of this was Lila's fault. She put her hand on her friend's slim brown wrist.

"I really am sorry," she said honestly. "We *are* friends, Lila. I'm just ... having a hard time at the moment with everything."

"Are you sure there's nothing else?" Lila's gaze

flicked towards Ollie, and she looked troubled. "I know you aren't Ollie's biggest fan, but can't you try to get along with him for my sake?"

"I don't dislike Ollie," Polly said helplessly. "It's just—"

There was a piercing scream from the back of the yacht. The whole boat stilled.

"You—!"

Rhi was clawing at Eve like a wildcat. Doing her best to fend off Rhi's whirling blows, Eve was ducking and fighting back with everything she had.

Looking rumpled and shaken, Max was trying to intervene, holding his hands up for peace. "Rhi, stop it! You can't just—"

"Don't you *dare* tell me what I can and can't do!" Rhi screamed. Her hand connected with Max's cheek with such a ringing slap that he shouted with pain and stumbled backwards. "I trusted you! And all the time you were . . . you were. . . !"

Rhi rounded on Eve again with a shriek of unhappiness.

"Stop it!" Eve hissed, trying to defend herself from Rhi's fists. "Someone's going to get hurt."

"Yes," Rhi said desperately. She struck herself on the chest. "Me. *I* got hurt. Your *friend*! Didn't our friendship mean anything to you?"

"What's wrong?" Lila said, moving swiftly to Rhi's side. "What's happened?"

Max was cowering behind Eve, who stood her ground looking defiant.

"Eve," Rhi wept. "Eve and . . . and Max. I caught them together in Eve's room. K . . . kissing."

Lila's face was a picture of horror. "Seriously?"

People were whispering and moving around the deck. Half the group drifted towards Eve and Max, looking watchful and wary. Polly stayed with the ones gathering around Rhi and offering comfort.

"You take whatever you want, don't you, Eve?" Lila said, fixing Eve with such a burning stare Polly half-expected Eve to burst into flames. "Whoever gets hurt. What a *special* person you are."

"Loving the protective vibe, Lila. Very macho," said Eve. If it hadn't been Eve, Polly could have sworn there were tears in her eyes. "Life's tough sometimes, OK?" She almost looked bored. "Things get out of control and it's just what happens."

"Nothing just *happens*," Rhi whispered. "People *make* things happen. Evil people like you."

Eve shrugged and sauntered away down the boat. Max followed, looking uncertainly over his shoulder at Rhi. Rhi wouldn't meet his eye.

"Show's over," said Ollie, clapping his hands. "Can someone put on some decent music? It's like a funeral round here."

It took a while for the party to loosen up again. A few people started dancing, but most went into huddles to discuss what had happened, staring at Rhi and whispering behind their hands. Polly felt terrible as she followed Lila, Rhi and Ollie down to the privacy of the cabin. She should have told Rhi what she had seen on Friday.

"Those two aren't worth your tears," she said, hugging Rhi tightly and trying to overcome her feelings of guilt. "Really. Forget about them."

"That's easy for you to say," Rhi sniffed.

"We'll be back on shore soon," said Ollie, looking out of the window. "So if we're planning on making Eve and Max walk the plank, we need to hurry up."

"Tactful as ever, Ollie," Lila said irritably as Rhi

burst into tears again. "It's OK, Rhi. Cry as much as you want."

Everyone tensed as Eve entered the cabin. She was smoothing her hair back over her head, her eyes flicking around the room.

"I want to speak to Rhi," she said. "In private. No one else needs to be here."

Seeing Eve standing there as if she had done nothing wrong triggered something in Polly. She walked right up to Eve, almost pushing her against the cabin wall.

"You have nothing to say that Rhi wants to hear," she said evenly.

Eve rolled her eyes. "I only want to talk to her. Isn't that how peace talks go? You *talk*?"

"Tell her to go away," Rhi wept.

"Ollie?" said Lila, rubbing Rhi's back. "Show Eve the door."

"I know where the door is, thanks," Eve said coldly. "It's my door, after all." She lowered her voice so that only Polly could hear. "This is all your fault. Spouting off the way you did."

Polly's heart thumped uncomfortably. "*I* wasn't kissing Max!"

Eve's eyes glittered like steel. "Rhi would never have caught us if you hadn't made her suspicious. I'll get even," she said in a silky whisper. "Don't think I won't."

"Are you still here?" Lila said pointedly from the other side of the cabin.

Eve stalked out, her jewelled sandals clinking on the wooden steps leading back to the deck. Polly swallowed. In that moment, even California didn't feel far enough away from Eve and her madness.

THIRTEEN

"So the train for London leaves at nine-thirty, OK?" Lila instructed Polly down the phone the next day. "We're going to have a total girly day, just you, me and Rhi. I'm going to take you to all my favourite London places, so you can forget about Heartside drama for a while. I have so much to show you. We're going to—"

"Can you hang up now?" Polly interrupted, half laughing. "It's already eight o'clock and I haven't thought about what I'm going to wear yet, let alone had any breakfast, so I need to get started. I'll see you at the station at nine-fifteen. Are we done?"

"I really want you and Rhi to relax today," Lila said earnestly. "We're going to find some cute boys for Rhi to look at and talk about so she can wipe that loser

Max from her head, and we're going to steer clear of any conversations about parents, and we're going to do some serious shopping, and we're going to catch up with each other properly. There are some awesome vintage shops that you are going to *love*. We are going to have so much fun!"

For the first time in ages, Polly felt genuinely excited. She didn't go to London very often, and with Lila and Rhi – both from London themselves – she knew she was going to have a really good time. "Understood, Captain, sir," she said, saluting her bedroom wall.

"Don't tease me, I'm serious," Lila insisted. "Nine-thirty, Polly! Don't do what you did on the dock yesterday and make me catch you from a moving train."

"I'm hanging up."

"Nine-thir—"

"Hanging up now!" Polly put down her phone, smiling.

The familiar dread began as she opened her wardrobe. Dress or trousers? Heels or flats? She wished she'd dyed her hair last night. She should have gone blond.

After fifteen minutes, Polly ran down the stairs in pink cigarette pants, a slim-fitting black jumper and her favourite faux-leather brogues. As she stood by the toaster, she studied her shoes. She could see her reflection in their shiny tips, and it wasn't good. She would have to change.

She took her toast back upstairs and started her outfit again. Mustard-yellow skirt this time, and a slightly sheer white shirt, and the yellow and white daisy earrings from the party on the boat. No sooner had she put the earrings on than she took them off again. She couldn't wear them today. They reminded her too much of that horrible afternoon.

The only other earrings she liked right now were a big pair of blue triangle ones. They didn't match the yellow skirt, or the pink cigarette pants, or the black jumper. They didn't match anything. Why had she bought them?

At nine o'clock, Polly was paralysed in the middle of her room, wearing her underwear, her triangle earrings, her make-up and nothing else. The nasty little voice was clamouring in her head: nothing matched, nothing suited her.

She forced herself to pull a long dark blue maxi skirt from the cupboard, and a silvery T-shirt. She slipped her feet back into her brogues and headed purposefully for the top of the stairs. It was a ten-minute walk to the station. She couldn't miss the train.

What is wrong with me? she thought in despair as she hesitated at the top of the stairs. The urge to examine herself in the mirror again was overpowering.

She returned to her room and wriggled back into her pink cigarette pants, the silver T-shirt and a fake leather jacket she'd customized with silver braid. With a chunky necklace she could get away without any earrings today. Brogues, check. Bag, check. Make-up, check.

You have to leave now, Polly ordered herself, putting the blue earrings neatly on her dresser.

Pausing hopelessly at the top of the stairs again, she closed her eyes. She had read somewhere about not pressuring yourself when you felt stressed. By choosing the right words, she could empower herself and leave her worries behind.

You want to leave, she thought, breathing slowly. *You are choosing to leave.*

She made it through the front door, pulling it behind her with a click. *I am choosing this*, she thought over and over again as she broke into a gentle jog, her bag bouncing by her side. It felt good.

Rhi said very little on the train, but Lila made up for it with her enthusiastic chatter.

"We'll start in Camden. You remember we used to go there years ago, Rhi? All those awesome market stalls? There's this fantastic jewellery place that does recycled beads that you'll love, Polly. And they do these amazing veggie hot dogs by the canal. I think they call them veggie bean dogs or something. I think I should warn you, though, they make me fart really badly."

Rhi gave a little snort. Grinning, Lila squeezed her hand and offered her a Haribo.

"Remind me not to sit next to you on the way home," Polly said, laughing.

Camden was around twenty minutes on the tube from the station. The tube was crowded with kids around their own age, and the chatter was loud and cheerful. Polly held her bag against her belly, leaned back against the window and listened to Lila describing her favourite shop.

"It's awesome because there are these new designers that no one's ever heard of, and their clothes are amazing but really cheap, and you can be the only person wearing their stuff and everyone's, 'Wow, where did you get that?' and you can smile mysteriously and be this unique fashion person."

"Polly's that already," Rhi said with a quiet smile.

Polly felt ridiculously pleased. She put one arm round Rhi's waist and the other round Lila's. Lila was right, as usual. They *were* going to have fun today.

Camden was full of cobbles and steps, brightly painted canal boats, street musicians and even more awesome vintage shops and market stalls than Lila had described. Polly bought a bag of old buttons from one stall, and an embroidered silk bag from a vintage shop, and a pair of large silver earrings shaped like birds which she put straight in her ears. Rhi limited herself to a neat brown leather bag stamped with little bones while Lila heaped her arms with T-shirts and bangles.

"Thank God Ollie didn't come," Lila gasped, as at last they staggered into a café near the canal and dumped their bags under a free table by the window. "He would have moaned the *whole* morning."

Polly's heart jumped at the mention of Ollie. She smoothed her hair behind her ears, and felt her new earrings brush against her fingers.

"He's great and everything, but I would have murdered him by about eleven o'clock," Lila added. "Boys and shopping don't go, do they?"

"Max—" Rhi started, then stopped almost at once. Polly realized it was the first time Rhi had mentioned her ex-boyfriend all morning. "Is an idiot?" she suggested, laying her vintage buttons out in a neat row on the table in size order.

Rhi smiled bravely. "When I saw Max with Eve on the boat yesterday, it was like. . . I can't even describe what it was like," she said with a sigh. "It was like he had ripped my heart out of my chest and stamped on it."

"Ouch," said Lila, shaking her head.

"I mean, Eve is really pretty and everything," Rhi went on, "so I understand why Max did it. But Eve will get bored of him soon. Then I'll win him back and everything will be fine again." She looked hopefully at the others.

Polly couldn't believe what she was hearing. Rhi wanted Max *back*? After what he'd done?

Lila almost choked over her sandwich. "Are you *insane*?" From the look on her face, she felt the same as Polly. "Why would you want that two-timing creep back in your life?"

"You deserve someone so much better than Max," said Polly, willing Rhi to see reason. "Someone who'll never hurt you like he did."

Rhi's eyes got watery. "The trouble is, I don't want anyone better. I just want him."

They finished their smoothies and packed their shopping into their shoulder bags. The mood had changed somehow. Thoughts of Eve and Max had spoiled things.

"Whoa, things just got busy," said Lila, stopping dead as they came out of the café. "What's going on?"

A flood of people surged down the road, carrying banners and slogans and chanting something. Police officers in hi-vis jackets had materialized on the street corners, looking watchful as the crowd swelled and pushed and shouted.

Polly pressed herself back against the café door, trying not to get jostled. She stared at the placards being held high in the air.

SHARE OUR WORLD! said one. CLEAN AIR, CLEAN SEA, CLEAN SOUL, said another. It was some kind of environmental protest.

Polly suddenly realized she was alone. Rhi and Lila had got caught up in the crowd, leaving her behind on the pavement.

"Wait!"

She stumbled into the road, trying to avoid the press of bodies and catch up with the others. It was impossible. All she could see was backs and feet, and all she could hear was the blast from the loudhailers all around her. She spun back, feeling frightened. The café and the pavement were already some distance away.

And she couldn't see Lila or Rhi at all.

FOURTEEN

Polly was in a state of terror. There were too many people. . . She was going to have a panic attack right here, in the middle of the road. . .

And then she saw Sam.

He was walking a short distance ahead of her, the shape of his head distinct against a bright placard scrawled with a bright red peace sign.

It can't be, she thought wildly. *I'm imagining things.*

The guy was the right height, and his hair was cut the way she remembered Sam's was on Friday. The collar of a cherry-red polo shirt peeked over the top of his jacket. It was him, she would swear it. But how could it be? They were in London, miles from

Heartside Bay. It was impossible that Sam would be here.

"SAVE OUR SEALS!" someone shouted down a loudhailer beside her. The blast of sound nearly made her leap out of her skin. *Seals*.

Polly came to life.

"Sam!" she screamed, fighting through the line of people marching in front of her. "SAM! Over here!"

Look back, she prayed, trying not to tread on people's toes, holding on to her bag like a lifejacket, jabbed by arms and placards on all sides. Posters of seals waved over her head. *Please look back. . .*

She stumbled sideways, catching her foot on an uneven cobble. Holding out her arms, she tried to right herself. If she fell, she would knock people over. *We'll all go down like skittles*, she thought a little hysterically.

"Save our seals!" roared the crowd, their feet stomping down the street in rhythm with their chanting. "Don't seal their fate!"

Someone caught her arm and pulled her upright. Stammering her thanks, she almost choked as she realized who had caught her.

Sam's face was a picture of disbelief. "Polly?"

Polly could feel a smile splitting her face in half. She was so pleased to see him, she couldn't speak. He was every bit as handsome as she remembered. "Sam!" she managed. "Yes, it's me. I. . . What are you *doing* here?"

"It's our protest," said Sam, looking stunned. "The one I told you about on Friday. We're marching on Parliament because they're debating the bill today. Are you really here or is this a mermaid trick?"

His arm came round her, protecting her from the crush of the crowd. Polly sank against him, smelling his familiar smell. "I'm really here," she said breathlessly. "I was shopping, and I got separated from my friends, and caught up in this – and then I saw you."

"You saw me," Sam repeated. He laughed in amazement, as if he still couldn't believe she was there. "I'm so sorry about Friday. The boat came loose – I hadn't moored it properly; I was a little . . . distracted, shall we say?"

Polly felt her cheeks getting hot at the look he gave her.

"And I was waiting on the beach for you and out of the corner of my eye I suddenly saw the boat drifting away, so I swam out to it, and that's when I got caught by the current."

"Were you OK?" said Polly, feeling alarmed.

He grinned, patting himself down. "Well, I still appear to be alive. Of course, a dodgy current wouldn't have been a problem for you, would it, mermaid?"

Polly could hardly take it in. He hadn't left on purpose. His boat had drifted, and he'd been caught in the current. And now he was here, beside her, holding her.

"You wouldn't believe how hard I tried to find you," he said, tightening his arm around her. "Apparently there are hundreds of Pollys in Heartside. I tried your school but they were closed for half-term. I tried everything." He looked at her in wonder. "And now here you are."

"Here I am," she agreed, laughing. "Mermaid magic. I swam up the canal, didn't I say?"

He wrapped her in a hug. Polly wanted time to stop, so she could enjoy the feel of his arms round her for ever.

"So where are your friends, then?" he said, letting go.

"I don't know," Polly confessed. "You're taller than

me. Can you see them in the crowd? Lila has a pink jacket on, and Rhi's is blue."

"Come this way." Sam took her hand and towed her to the side of the road. Standing a little higher on the raised pavement, Polly scanned the crowd with one hand shading her eyes, with Sam beside her doing the same. She still felt as if she were in a dream.

"There's someone in a pink jacket by the statue over there," said Sam suddenly.

Polly saw Lila the moment Lila saw her. They exchanged arm waves. *Wait until Rhi and Lila see who I'm with*, Polly thought, wanting to hug herself with delight.

Sam pulled her back into the crowd. "Excuse us, excuse us, mermaid coming through, they do so much wonderful work for the seals, you know," he said, grinning back at Polly as they pushed through the crush. "Excuse us!"

"Polly!" Lila flew at her and hugged her so hard Polly thought her ribs were going to crack. "You gave me such a fright. One minute you were there and the next. . ." She trailed off, and looked at Sam in surprise. "Who are you?"

"Hi," said Sam politely. He ran his hand through his short hair, making it stick up and look even cuter. "I'm Sam, pleased to meet you."

Lila's mouth dropped open. "Sam?" She looked at Polly. "Wait, *the* Sam? Sam with the boat?"

Polly could feel herself blushing all over. "Sam from last week, yes. We just bumped into each other."

Lila folded her arms and grinned. "Well, well," she said, looking at Sam's long legs and wide shoulders. "It looks like you're real after all. And very nice too."

"Lila," Polly protested, laughing.

"What?" said Lila, grinning wickedly.

A warm smile spread across Rhi's face as Polly explained who Sam was. "Nice to meet you, Sam," she said shyly. "Thanks for reuniting us."

Sam squeezed Polly's hand. "Believe me, it was no hardship. Are you sticking around for a while?"

Lila looked regretful. "We need to catch a train home. Rhi has a crashing headache and I think we're all shopped out."

"I'd love to stay," Polly said honestly. "But I'm exhausted after everything and, to be honest, my feet are killing me."

"That's the trouble with being a mermaid," Sam said sympathetically.

Polly giggled at the mystification on Lila and Rhi's faces.

"I'm in town for the rest of the day with this protest," Sam said. "But I'll walk you all to the station?"

They found a quiet side street away from the crush, taking a back route that Sam seemed to know. Polly tightened her fingers round Sam's, wanting to hold on to him, feeling sad that she was going already but unbelievably happy at the same time. Now they had found each other, they would see each other again.

"Text me your number?" said Sam as they reached the tube.

Polly messaged him, her fingers trembling a little on the keys. Part of her didn't want to take her eyes off him in case he vanished again, like a mirage in the desert. He sent a message straight back.

Go and put your tail up, mermaid.
I'll call you.
Sam x

Lila and Rhi took a polite interest in the tube posters as Sam stroked the back of Polly's head, his fingers sliding through her hair.

"Can we meet tomorrow?" he asked.

"I'd like that," Polly said, smiling up at him.

And then he was kissing her again, lifting her off her feet and twirling her round.

"See you," he grinned as he put her down again. He raised a hand at Lila and Rhi. "Nice to meet you guys."

He put his hands in his pockets and sauntered away down the road. Polly watched him until he was out of sight, feeling happier than she had ever felt in her life.

FIFTEEN

True to his word, Sam called on Tuesday morning.

"How are the feet?"

"Good." Polly grinned down the phone. "How are the seals?"

"In ever more need of our help," Sam sighed. "We lost the debate. We made a good noise at the protest, though. And we're not defeated. We'll get the bill through in the end."

"I really hope you do," Polly said honestly.

"That's good to hear. Sometimes it feels like we're up against a brick wall."

He sounded downhearted. Polly wanted to cheer him up.

"Well, you know what they say about bricks," she said.

"What?"

"They're basically made of sand," Polly explained, and felt rewarded by his laughter on the other end.

"So we're just up against a massive sandcastle?"

"Yes. All you need to do is keep stomping."

"I like that," he said. "You're wise for a mermaid, aren't you?"

Polly felt warm all over at the admiration in his voice. And when he suggested they meet at one of her favourite cafés on the Marine Parade in half an hour, she agreed at once.

Somehow her outfit came together really easily today. She chose a red and blue chevron-patterned dress, with her brogues and her new silver bird earrings. Grabbing her favourite old faux-leather jacket from the peg in the hall, she flew out into the blustery morning without a backwards glance at the mirror in her wardrobe.

How could she even *think* about moving to California with her dad now that Sam was back in her life?

No sooner had the thought crossed Polly's mind than she felt annoyed with herself. She had always laughed at girls who dropped everything for a boy. But it was hard to remember her plans for the future when all she could think about was Sam, and the way his eyes crinkled at the corners when he smiled, and the way his lips felt on hers.

He was waiting for her at a corner table with a large mug of tea, a sky-blue shirt and a big smile. He got up at once, and kissed her in a way that made her head start spinning. Being in his arms felt so *right*.

"You look completely beautiful this morning," he said when he released her. "I love what you do with your clothes."

"Fish scales are easier," she said, grinning. "They go with *everything*."

The wind howled on the beach outside the fogged-up café window, but sitting snuggled on a padded bench with Sam's arm round her and a mug of hot peppermint tea, Polly didn't notice.

"Did you really go to my school to find me?" she asked shyly.

He put his hand on his heart. "I swear. And Facebook. And Twitter. And the phone book."

Polly took a thoughtful sip of her peppermint tea. "What were the chances of bumping into each other in London like that, do you think?"

"About a million to one." He took her hand and kissed her palm and Polly thought she might die of happiness.

They talked about the seals again, then moved on to the melting ice caps and the problems with shale gas fracking. Sam had strong opinions on all of it, and she loved that he cared so much.

"Humans are wrecking the world," he said, shaking his head. "You know that Gandhi quote? 'Be the change you want to see'? That's what I'm trying to do. I'm trying to be the change."

Polly had never known a boy who she could talk to about really important issues the way she could talk to Sam. He was smart, and interested in her opinion, and his kisses made her melt. How could she take up her dad's offer of a life in California now she'd found him again? But was she mad to consider not moving, just for the sake of a boy? It went against everything she believed in. She felt hopelessly confused.

"You've gone very quiet," Sam commented. "Is everything OK?"

Polly forced a smile. "Yes, sorry. What were you saying?"

"I was telling you about the fund-raising event at Heartwell Manor tomorrow evening," he said. "You know, the smart hotel in the east of town?"

Polly did know it. She'd walked past its grand windows and elegant gardens a hundred times, but she'd never been inside.

"There will be a lot of influential people there, who might donate to our seal project," Sam went on. "I have two tickets. Would you be my date?"

Polly felt consumed with delight. "I'd love to!"

He beamed. "I'll pick you up at seven-thirty tomorrow evening. Now let's go for a walk on the beach. I want to kiss you as close to the sea as I can."

Polly couldn't wait to get started on her outfit for Heartwell Manor. It had to be something really special for tomorrow night.

She made a quick trip to her favourite charity shop in the Old Town on Tuesday afternoon. It specialized in vintage things that needed a little extra love to bring them back to life, and there was always something to catch Polly's eye.

She saw what she wanted immediately. A full-length

dress in gold and black brocade, with a nipped-in waist and a neat bow at the back, from maybe the fifties or sixties. It was too long for her as usual, and the side zip was broken. She paid for it, went to another shop a few doors down for thread and a new zip, and hurried home.

The first thing to do was cut the dress down to size. Taking a deep breath – this was always the scariest part – Polly snipped the fabric away. Then she pinned and hemmed it to knee length. She gave it a quick press and tried it on for length, twirling carefully in front of the mirror, checking that nothing was too long or too short. Perfect.

She had chosen a bright blue zip, liking the contrast with the gold brocade. It was fiddly, but when she had finished, the dress slid on and fitted her to perfection.

Not bad, she thought happily, studying her reflection. She would put a blue stripe in her hair to pick up on the bright blue zip, she decided, and add some extra blue ribbon on the bow at the back to bring everything together. With her high-heeled blue shoes and a small gold clutch, she would be

Sam's perfect date for what promised to be a perfect evening.

Sam's eyes widened as Polly opened the door at seven-thirty on Wednesday evening.

"Wow," he said, his eyes fixed on the gold and blue shimmer of her dress. "Where did you get your outfit? It's extraordinary."

"I made it," she said, pushing her new blue stripe of hair behind one ear. Suddenly feeling worried, she added: "Good extraordinary or bad extraordinary?"

"Very good extraordinary," he said. He put his hands on her neat brocade waist and kissed her gently on her coral-coloured lips. "You will blow them all away."

"You look great too," Polly said, smiling up at him. "The tux is very James Bond."

He tweaked his bow tie and his cuffs, and smoothed down the black satin on his lapels. "Only the best for you," he said, smiling. "Ready to go?"

It was a twenty-minute walk across town to Heartwell Manor. Holding Sam's hand and snuggled inside her favourite faux-fur jacket, Polly hardly noticed. He was full of energy tonight, talking non-stop about the plans he had for the evening.

"Everyone who's anyone is going tonight. If I play this right, I could raise a lot of money for the seals."

"Who's hosting it?" Polly asked as they walked.

"Mayor Somerstown."

Polly almost stumbled on the kerb. "Mayor *Somerstown*?"

"Do you know him?" Sam said, looking at her.

Polly wanted to die. A glamorous party thrown by Eve's father? Eve would be there for sure. Maybe with Max. The thought made her feel a little ill.

"I know his daughter," she said.

Sam brightened. "Excellent! Can you introduce me? Mayor Somerstown is an influential man around here. He could be just the kind of person to back our cause."

Heartwell Manor glinted at them in the dark of the evening, strung about with lights and lit with flares down the drive. Big cars were swinging up to the front door, disgorging elegant men and women in gorgeous designer outfits. Polly tugged nervously at her dress, suddenly feeling completely inadequate. She'd never seen so many elegant people gathered in one place in her whole life.

"You'll be fine," Sam said, noticing her nerves as they approached the front door. "You look a million dollars." And he kissed her encouragingly on the cheek.

Sam seemed completely at ease. He probably went to events like this all the time, Polly thought. His private school clearly gave him an extra layer of confidence. Her own confidence was feeling a little thin.

The sounds of a string quartet floated in the candlelit hallway. People were talking and laughing, holding glasses of champagne everywhere Polly looked. The women's outfits were even more amazing close up.

"What on earth are you doing here, Polly?" said a familiar, drawling voice.

Eve was wearing a long column-style dress of dark blue satin with matching shoes. Her red hair fell sleekly on her shoulders, and small, clear gemstones winked in her ears. Polly knew without asking that they were real diamonds.

"Interesting outfit," said Eve, smirking as she scanned Polly's dress. "Unique, you might say. But we can always rely on you for that."

In her brightly coloured dress with its mismatched zip, Polly suddenly felt like a Christmas cracker. She nodded, wishing she had worn something else. Why did Eve always make her feel this way?

"She's with me," said Sam. He held out his hand. "Sam Evans. How do you do?"

Eve shook hands, looking Sam up and down with her glittering grey eyes. "Eve Somerstown," she said, smiling. "Goodness, he's lovely, isn't he," she said to Polly, as if Sam wasn't there. "Wherever did you find him?"

Polly couldn't help remembering Eve's last words to her. *I'll get even. Don't think I won't.*

"On the beach," she blurted.

On the beach? She'd made Sam sound like a seashell.

"It's a wonderful party," said Sam. He looked around the room. "Your father is a very generous man."

"These things are never about the host's generosity," said Eve, waving carelessly at the beautiful lighting, the waiters with their silver trays of canapés and the lilting sounds of the string quartet. "It's about the generosity of his guests. Don't you find?"

"I know how hard fundraising can be," Sam agreed. "I'm trying to find sponsors for my coastal project, protecting the seals, actually. Perhaps you know some people I could talk to?"

"Absolutely," said Eve. To Polly's horror, she slid a slim arm through the crook of Sam's elbow. "Come and meet my father. I'm sure he can introduce you to someone useful. You don't mind if I borrow him for a bit, do you, Polly."

As usual with Eve, it wasn't a question. What could she say? *Yes, I do mind?*

"I won't be long," Sam promised as Eve pulled him away through the crowd, leaving Polly alone by a tray of champagne.

This is for Sam's cause, Polly told herself, trying to smile and look as if she was OK standing there by herself. *I can't get in the way of that, even if it means he has to spend time with Eve.* She didn't like how Eve had looked at Sam as though he was something delicious to eat.

She took a glass of orange juice from a nearby tray and drank it. Then, after a short while walking around the grand rooms of the hotel trying to find Sam, she set down her glass on a window sill and headed into the garden.

It was dark and cool out here. Flares lit the corners of the garden, and several other people were strolling about in the darkness, arm in arm. Polly felt more alone than ever. She fiddled with her clutch, and tried not to panic about the zip on her dress, which suddenly felt loose. The music drifted through the trimmed hedges, light and elegant.

Her father's farm wouldn't be like this, she thought, trailing her fingers across the tops of the neatly trimmed privet hedges. It would be wild and natural, full of flowers and wildlife. She had a feeling any rabbits or squirrels that dared to appear in the Heartwell Manor gardens were immediately chased away by the army of gardeners. She closed her eyes, imagining the warmth of the California sun on her skin.

"Oh, sorry!"

She stopped, mortified. She had almost crashed into a couple embracing by the elegant stone fountain in the centre of the garden.

Then she realized who it was.

SIXTEEN

Polly froze in horror as Sam pulled away from Eve's arms. Eve smoothed her hair and straightened her dress.

"Well, it's been fun," she said, casually wiping a speck of lipstick from Sam's cheek. "We must do it again some time."

Polly could hardly breathe. Her boyfriend and her worst enemy? It was impossible. They had only just met! Hadn't they? Was this a set-up? Was Sam a two-timing creep like Max? How far would he go to get his sponsorship for the seals? Her mind raced through all the possible explanations, desperate to find a way out. But there was just this: Eve, and Sam, in the dark. Kissing.

Sam looked pale. "Polly, it's not what it looks like—"

"I know what I saw, Sam," she managed to say. She wondered if she was going to be sick right at Sam's feet.

"Polly, please believe me," he said hurriedly, looking at Eve. "Eve surprised me. I didn't know she would kiss me!"

Even in the darkness, Polly could see Eve's eyes glittering with triumph. *I'll get even. Don't think I won't.*

"This is all very dramatic for just one little kiss." Eve patted her hair again and sighed. "Take it from me, Sam. You can do so much better than Polly. Why would you want to be second choice anyway?"

Sam looked even more confused and worried. "What do you mean, second choice?"

"You'll have to ask Polly that," said Eve silkily.

Polly burst into tears. She could feel her mascara running in black rivers down her face. Her heart lay in splinters on the grass. Eve's victory was complete.

"I hate you, Sam. And I never want to see you again," she wept.

"Polly!" Sam shouted after her.

Polly had spun round and run back up the garden. Twigs and branches scraped viciously at her arms and legs, but she hardly noticed. The image of Sam kissing Eve was burned into her memory. She had to leave or she would fall down in a dead faint.

There was the sound of running feet behind her. Someone caught her by the elbow and yanked her round.

"You have to believe me, Polly," begged Sam. His bowtie was half undone. Polly wondered if Eve had untied it. Eve had ruined *everything*.

"I'm going home," she said, wrenching her arm away from him.

"Give me a chance to explain! *She* kissed *me*!"

"It didn't look that way to me," Polly wept.

"It's true." Sam took her arm again, more gently. "Please, Polly, calm down. Can we talk about this?"

Polly took several deep, trembling breaths. She wanted to believe him. It would be typical of Eve, getting back at her in this way. Making her think the worst of Sam.

"She really kissed *you*?" she said at last, wiping her eyes with trembling fingers. "And you weren't expecting it?"

"Yes," Sam insisted. "She said there was someone I should meet out in the garden, so like an idiot I followed her. You saw the rest."

Polly closed her eyes. "I'm sorry," she said, still fighting to keep calm. "I believe you."

Sam pulled her into a grateful hug. After a moment's resistance, Polly clung to him like he was a life raft and they were back in the sea again. He kissed her cheeks, and brushed away her tears with the pad of his thumb.

"Eve's so awful," Polly hiccupped. "She's cheating with her best friend's boyfriend at the moment."

Sam whistled. "So am I forgiven?"

Polly sniffed and nodded. "You're forgiven."

They stood with their arms round each other in the dark garden, in the glowing light from the hotel windows. Polly rested her head against his warm chest, and closed her eyes, and wished they were back by the sea beside a driftwood campfire.

"What did Eve mean," Sam said into her hair, "about me being your second choice?"

Polly tensed. *You really knew what you were doing, didn't you, Eve?* she thought. It wasn't enough just to kiss Sam. She had to make him doubt Polly as well.

"Just another of Eve's lies," she said.

"Really?" Sam looked at her with dark eyes. "Because if there's someone else. . ."

"There isn't," Polly interrupted. She was desperate for him to believe her. Ollie couldn't come between them like a ghost now. "Really, Sam. Eve just made that up to make you doubt me. She hates me because I know about her and this guy she's seeing behind her friend's back. I've never felt this way about anyone but you."

He looked relieved. "Anyone who can pull a stunt like the one she just tried in the garden can't be trusted. I can see that. I'm mad about you, Polly. I couldn't bear to lose you over a bunch of lies. Can we forget this ever happened?"

He kissed her again. Polly sank against him and kissed him back with all her heart.

"Let's get out of here," he said at last. "Thinking about that girl is making my skin crawl. You look beautiful tonight, Polly. Let's go into town. How about the Heartbeat Café?"

"Aren't we a bit formal?" said Polly with a giggle.

"The Heartbeat will love us," Sam promised.

Polly fixed her ruined make-up in the bathroom as quickly as she could. There were wipes, and moisturizer beside the sinks, and she had put some extra mascara and lipstick into her clutch. Knowing Sam was waiting for her made her feel calmer, and she resisted the urge to check and double-check her dress. Ten minutes later, Sam had helped her into her faux-fur jacket and they were walking down into the Old Town together.

The Heartbeat glowed like an old jewel in the dark February evening, lights flickering cheerfully in its windows. Heartwell Manor had been beautiful, but cold too, like a grand old queen. The Heartbeat felt more like the jolly-faced cook down in the queen's castle kitchens, warm and welcoming.

People looked at them curiously as they came through the door in their evening finery. Polly's heart almost burst with pride when Sam gave her a warm smile, and held her hand, and made it clear that they were together. They were definitely the most stylish couple in the room.

"Polly!"

Lila was waving enthusiastically from one the tables

near the stage. Polly's smile faltered as she clocked Ollie's blond head beside her best friend.

"There's your friend," Sam said, nodding in Lila's direction. "Shall we join her?"

Joining Lila and Ollie was the last thing Polly wanted to do. Ollie was looking extra gorgeous this evening in a chunky green jumper that brought out the blue in his eyes and emphasized his wide shoulders. Her stomach fluttered uncomfortably.

"Can't we sit by ourselves?" she began, but Sam was already leading her across the room.

"You guys look amazing," said Lila in wonder as they reached the table. "Polly, your dress is incredible. You look like a model. Where have you been?"

"To a very boring party" said Sam. He offered his hand to Ollie. "Hi, I'm Sam."

"Ollie," Ollie grunted.

Instead of shaking Sam's hand, he shoved his own hands into his pockets and stared at the table. He clearly thought Sam was a posh idiot in a tux, not worth getting to know. Polly's stomach tied itself into unhappy knots.

"Ignore him," Lila said, shooting a glare at Ollie.

"He was playing football and lost and is taking it out on everyone he meets tonight."

"Who do you support, then?" Ollie threw at Sam.

"Seals, mainly," said Sam with a smile.

Ollie frowned. "Is that a local team?"

Polly wanted to die. A sweat was breaking out across her back and pooling unpleasantly in her armpits. How long would they have to stay here?

"We were about to go home," Lila was saying. "But why don't we meet tomorrow night for a proper double date?"

"I don't think we can," Polly said. *Say we can't*, she willed Sam. *Say we already have plans.*

"Of course you can," Lila insisted. "I want to get to know Sam better now you two are going out. We'll have a great time. Won't we, Ollie?"

"Whatever," sighed Ollie.

"That would be great, Lila," said Sam politely. "We'd love it."

Polly wanted the floor to open up and swallow her. A whole evening with Ollie and Sam? It was guaranteed to be awful.

SEVENTEEN

"But we won't be able to talk properly," complained Lila on the phone later that night, when Polly suggested they should spend their double date at the cinema the following evening. "Why don't we just have a meal together?"

Not talking is the whole point, Polly thought. An evening where they could avoid too much conversation was definitely the best way to go. "It's a really great film, Lila," she said in her most persuasive voice. "I've been meaning to see it for ages. And we'll have time to talk beforehand. We could book a table at a nice restaurant before the film. Where would you like to go?"

"Luigi's?" said Lila. She sounded brighter. "It's

not far from the cinema and they do awesome pizzas. Italian's good for veggies. Is Sam a veggie too?"

"Yes," said Polly, smiling. It was yet another thing she loved about her boyfriend. He cared too much about the world to eat its animals.

"There'll be plenty of meaty boy pizzas for Ollie," said Lila, "so he should be OK, so long as we don't make him eat any salad. I'm really sorry he was so rude to Sam earlier. He was in a funny mood all evening, to be honest." She sighed. "I don't understand him sometimes."

"Don't worry about it,' said Polly. "Sam hardly noticed."

This wasn't quite true. Polly had apologized to Sam over and over for Ollie's strange behaviour as they walked home. Sam had insisted that Polly should forget it.

"He's probably jealous that I've got such a gorgeous girlfriend," he said, laughing.

Polly squirmed uncomfortably. If only that were true.

"He's OK normally," she said, wondering why she was defending Ollie.

138

"I can put up with him for Lila's sake," Sam had answered, tightening his arm round Polly's shoulders. "She's great, isn't she?"

For some reason, this hadn't made Polly feel much better.

"So if the film starts at eight, we should book Luigi's for, what, six-thirty?" Lila was saying. "It's only a ten-minute walk to the cinema from there. This is going to be great, Polly. And if Ollie's an idiot again, you have my permission to kick him under the table!"

So now it was Thursday, and already six-fifteen. Polly was back on the brink of panic, fighting through her wardrobe with the usual sensation of falling from a great height. She'd tried on a million outfits. At last, Polly made it outside to where Sam was waiting for her, looking tall and handsome and relaxed.

"Sorry," she gasped, fighting the mad desire to return to the mirror for one final outfit check. "I'm really sorry. We probably have to run now."

Luigi's was on the edge of town, not far from Heartside Bay's small four-screen cinema. Polly's face was running with sweat as she and Sam came through the doors at twenty to seven. She had spent ages getting the perfect flick with her eyeliner so that her eyes looked huge and fairy-like, but she could already feel her make-up clumping in the corners of her eyes and her hair clinging sweatily to the back of her neck. She probably looked like a clown, not a fairy at all.

No change there, she thought glumly.

Lila and Ollie were waiting at a small curved booth with a padded bench running all the way round it. The way they were sitting suggested to Polly that they had been arguing. She wondered why.

"You're here!" Lila said, sounding relieved. "It's great, isn't it? They're bringing us some breadsticks and sparkling water – is that OK?"

Polly studied the table, feeling worried. It was very small. They would be cramped together like sardines in a tin. And if Sam did his usual thing and let her sit down first, she would have to wriggle in beside Ollie, which she really didn't want to do.

"After you," said Sam, as Polly had known he would.

She swallowed unhappily, and squeezed on to the padded bench next to Ollie, tugging down her sequinned miniskirt so that it didn't ride too far up her legs. He looked at her with stormy blue eyes. Polly couldn't decide if he was pleased to see her or not.

"Hi," she said nervously.

"Hi yourself," Ollie replied.

Sam settled in on Polly's other side, nodding briefly at Ollie. Ollie half-lifted his hand in return.

"This is fun already, isn't it?" said Lila brightly. "Sam, do you want something to drink, like soda or juice?"

"Water's fine, thanks," said Sam.

"What are you, a fish?" Ollie enquired, taking a long and noisy slurp from his glass of Coke.

Sam smiled sideways at Polly. "No. But coincidentally, Polly's a mermaid."

Ollie belched. "She looks pretty human to me," he said, glancing at Polly's outfit. "You know, for a disco-dancing pixie."

Polly flushed, horribly aware of Ollie's warmth pressing against her, all the way from her shoulders to her knees. She should have known her sparkly skirt was too dressy for a simple trip to the cinema.

"I'd prefer it if you didn't insult my girlfriend," said Sam evenly.

"What's so insulting about that?" Ollie protested. He patted Polly's sparkly thigh, almost making Polly leap out of her skin. "I happen to like pixies."

Lila caught Polly's eye apologetically. Polly grimaced back. This was going to be a long night.

Ollie started texting someone, making no effort to join in on Lila and Sam's awkward attempts at conversation. Polly's thigh burned with the memory of Ollie's warm hand. She wished it wouldn't. He was being horrible tonight. She should hate him. But she couldn't.

"Pizzas!" said Lila with relief as two waiters headed towards them, holding steaming plates high above their heads. "Yours is the goat's cheese and rocket one, right, Sam?"

Ollie snorted. "And the margherita covered in shredded pig is mine," he said. "In case you were wondering, veggie boy."

"I always prefer the veggie ones," said Lila heroically. "The flavours are much more interesting."

"Sure," said Ollie, nodding as he helped himself to a mountain of parmesan cheese from the bowl in the middle of the table. He added a squirt of ketchup to the middle of his pizza. "If you're a rabbit."

Polly took Sam's warm hand and tried to focus on the good things in her life right now. It was hard.

"Stop behaving like an idiot, Ollie," Lila snapped, struggling to control her temper.

Ollie draped his arm round the back of the padded bench behind Polly's head. She could sense its warmth near her shoulders. She gripped Sam's hand more tightly.

"I'm not the one who came up with this stupid double-date idea," Ollie objected. "What is this film, anyway? I bet there isn't a single decent action sequence. I'm missing some good telly for this."

Polly had to leave before she screamed. There was no way out of here except by crawling under the table. In a brief moment of desperation, she wondered if it was worth trying.

The waiter placed a large glass of apple juice beside her. Polly stared at it, and took a deep breath. Then she deliberately swept her arm across the table, as if reaching for the parmesan.

"Oh!"

Her shriek was genuine. The apple juice now soaking the front of her tank top and her skirt was cold and sticky. Sam leaped to his feet before the juice could splatter sideways. Ollie jumped up too, almost knocking his pizza to the floor in a bid to escape a soaking.

"I'm sorry," Polly stammered, wiping at her top. "My fault."

"Man, that went *everywhere*," Ollie laughed, mopping at the table with a handful of paper napkins.

"Don't worry, Polly," said Sam soothingly. "Accidents happen."

"You poor thing," said Lila in dismay. "Your top's a mess."

Polly had a genuine urge to cry. Even though she'd spilled her drink on purpose, it was still the most disgusting feeling, the way it was soaking right through her clothes. "I . . . I really am sorry," she said, wiping herself frantically with a napkin. "I have to go home and change. . ."

"I'll take you," Sam offered at once.

"Everyone loves a hero," sighed Ollie.

Polly wriggled free from the imprisoning table. Her face felt hot with a combination of shame and relief. She was as bad as Eve, engineering her so-called accident.

"We'll wait for you at the cinema, shall we?" said Lila anxiously as Sam threw a twenty-pound note on the table and helped Polly towards the door.

"Go ahead without us," said Polly, hating herself. "I'll have to see the film some other time. Thanks for arranging this evening, Lila. I'm sorry I messed it up. I hope you and Ollie have a good time."

The cold air outside was a welcome relief after the stifling atmosphere in the restaurant. Polly walked in silence with Sam for a while, and then sat down on a wall when it felt as if her legs were about to give way.

"I'm sorry for making such a mess," she mumbled.

"That was no accident," said Sam. He looked at her curiously.

Polly could feel exhausted tears welling up in her eyes. What must he think of her, pulling a stunt like that? As usual, she had ruined everything.

She couldn't do anything right.

EIGHTEEN

Sam gave a long, relieved whistle. "Quick thinking. I couldn't have stood it much longer."

Polly blinked back her tears. "You're not angry with me?"

He looked astonished. "Why would I be angry? If we'd stayed much longer, I might have punched that guy. I can't believe he called you a disco-dancing pixie!"

"He's a bit of a joker," Polly muttered. "He doesn't mean it."

"I'd rather have you to myself anyway," said Sam, pulling Polly off the wall and kissing her. "We'll be back at your house in fifteen minutes if we walk fast. When you've changed, we'll do something else instead."

The cold air against her wet clothes made Polly

shiver. Sam walked beside her, keeping her warm in the crook of his arm.

She didn't know what to think about Ollie's behaviour. She was glad they had escaped, but she was upset that he and Sam got along so badly. She wanted Sam to like him. She also wondered whether Lila was yelling at Ollie right now for spoiling the evening. Polly didn't want to think too hard about the way Lila and Ollie's relationship seemed to be cracking around the edges.

"You must be Sam," said Polly's mum brightly as they came in through the front door. "Polly's been talking about you for days."

Polly groaned to herself. *Thanks, Mum. Now I look really cool.*

"How do you do, Mrs Nelson," said Sam, holding out his hand.

Polly's mother's smile thinned. "It's Ms Allen these days," she said. "I'm sure Polly's told you all about the way her hopeless father ran out on us six years ago."

Sam looked embarrassed. "I'm sorry to hear that. We haven't really talked about our families much."

Polly wanted to disappear through the floorboards.

Could her mother ruin her life any further? "Sam doesn't want to hear any of that," she hissed. "I need to go upstairs and change." She looked at Sam. "Will you be OK waiting?"

"Of course he will," said her mum at once. "I'll look after him. We can get to know each other better, can't we, Sam?"

Polly fled up the stairs. The apple juice had dried now, and her clothes were sticking uncomfortably to her skin. She couldn't wait to get out of them and dive into a hot shower where she could scrub everything away. If only she could scrub the whole evening away as well.

She dreaded to think what her mother was telling Sam down in the kitchen. Would he think it was weird she hadn't mentioned how her parents were divorced? She felt as if she had been lying to him somehow. He was right about how they hadn't talked about their families. She didn't know a thing about his home life either.

She stood in the shower, shampooing her hair and conditioning it, washing herself with every product on the bathroom shelf. It was only when the water started running cold that she forced herself out of the shower and wearily studied her wardrobe for what to wear. Why was it always such a struggle?

Time was ticking. At last she pulled on the pink cigarette pants she'd worn to London together with a white jumper. They would have to do. If she left Sam alone with her mum for much longer, he'd never want to see her again.

Her phone rang as she was moving down the stairs. She yanked it out of her pocket, dreading a call from Lila asking if she had got home OK.

"Polly-Dolly! Great, I caught you. Are you busy?"

"Hey, Dad," said Polly, taking the treads on the stairs two at a time. "I'm kind of going out right now."

"Sounds fun." He dropped his voice meaningfully. "With anyone nice?"

Polly laughed. "Not telling you."

"Do you want to meet tomorrow? When would be a good time?"

By that, Polly guessed he meant "When will your mother be out?" The lightness she had been feeling at the sound of his voice wilted in her chest like old spinach. She stopped at the bottom of the stairs, fiddling absently with the handrail.

"Whenever," she said quietly.

"Why don't we say twelve? I'll pick you up—"

Polly's phone was abruptly snatched out of her hand.

"How many times must I tell you to leave her alone, Alex?" her mother hissed into the receiver, resting one hand on Polly's shoulder. "You can't see her, understand? I won't have you breaking her heart like you once broke mine."

Through waves of shame, Polly saw Sam standing very still in the kitchen doorway. Right at that moment, all she wanted to do was run back up the stairs and lock herself in the bathroom until the whole misery was over.

I'm sorry, she mouthed helplessly at Sam as her mother ranted on down the phone.

Forget about it, he mouthed back with a shrug. *Shall we go?*

It was the best idea Polly'd heard all evening. She grabbed a scarf from the hallstand and dragged Sam through the front door. Snatches of her parents' argument drifted through the door catch as she hustled him down the drive.

"Unreliable. . . Irresponsible. . . Thoughtless. . ."

Finally, blissfully, the sounds of arguing faded into the night.

"I'm really sorry about that," said Polly in a trembling voice. "My mother's a nightmare at the moment. Did she bore you to death in the kitchen while I was changing?"

Sam shook his head. "We talked mainly about school, actually."

His voice sounded funny. Polly felt crushed with anxiety. Would he hate her now he'd seen what her family was like?

"Everything was great between them once," she blurted. "It's amazing what six years can do. It's like they're at war, and I'm the prize."

They had reached the little park at the end of Polly's road. Sam held open the gate.

"Believe me, I know all about parents," he said.

Something in his tone of voice caught Polly's attention. He sounded sad.

"I'm going to challenge you to a swing-off," he said before she could ask him anything else. He jogged towards the set of swings which stood in the centre of the park. "Are you up for it?"

Polly laughed, feeling marginally more cheerful. "Definitely."

Sam's long legs made his swing go much higher than hers, even though she worked her legs like a blur to beat him. The moon shone overhead, casting strange shadows. Polly tipped her head back, feeling her hair swinging in the evening breeze just as it had done the first time she ever came to this park.

Sam flew off the swing and landed in a perfect commando roll on the ground. Polly flung herself from the swing after him. For just half a second she felt weightless, carefree.

"Nice landing action for a fish," said Sam, catching her as she hit the ground. "Roundabout next?"

They took turns pushing each other on the roundabout. Then one pushed and ran and jumped aboard with the other, holding on and laughing in the darkness.

"I'm so glad we didn't go and see that film," Polly said as they slowed to a squeaky halt. She swung her feet off the side of the roundabout.

"This is so much better," Sam agreed. "Cheap. Fun. Dark."

He gathered her in his arms and kissed her beneath the moon, their shadows striping the dark grass behind them. And Polly knew that Sam was completely perfect. Finally she had found someone to replace Ollie in her heart.

They left the roundabout and sat on a cool shadowy bench, side by side, their heads resting against each other.

"Do you find it hard?" Sam said into the darkness. "Having divorced parents?"

Polly remembered laughing with her parents round the kitchen table in San Francisco, sunlight pooling on the waxed kitchen floor at their feet. The memory swelled and threatened to burst.

"It's hard when I think about it," she said. "But most of the time, it's OK."

She sensed that he wanted to say something more. A dim recollection of how he had sounded when he told her he understood parents swam to the surface of her mind. She shifted round to see his face a little better.

"Why do you ask?"

Sam looked down at his hands. "My parents are getting divorced," he said. "It's going through at the moment."

Polly took his hands and held them. She of all people knew the pain that he was feeling. Further proof, if she needed it, of how perfect they were for each other.

"Are you going to live with your mum?" she asked. "Or your dad?"

"Mum."

"So where's your dad going?"

"Dad's not the one who's leaving town," Sam said.

A shard of ice pierced Polly's heart. "Your mother's leaving Heartside? And . . . and you're leaving Heartside with her?"

Sam squeezed her hand. "Mum's been offered an incredible job in government in London. To make the whole transition easier for me, she's arranged an apprenticeship for me with this amazing politician – a green campaigner who knows everything about environmental issues. He's exactly the kind of politician I want to be when I'm older."

Polly had the strangest sensation that the bench was breaking beneath her, and that she was falling.

"When are you leaving?" she whispered, dreading his answer.

He looked at her, willing her to understand. "I'm moving after half-term."

NINETEEN

No! Polly wanted to shout. After half-term . . . that was next week. Sam *couldn't* leave Heartside in just a few days' time. They'd only just found each other.

Why did everyone leave?

She gave a choking sob as an awful feeling of grief swept over her.

"Polly, please don't cry." Tears were glistening in Sam's eyes as well. "We'll be fine. London's not so far away. We'll still see each other."

"It's not enough!" Polly's heart was breaking all over again. "Long-distance relationships don't work, Sam. It's stupid to pretend they do."

She pulled her hands from Sam's grasp and ran towards the park gate.

"Don't go!" Sam ran after her, trying to pull her back towards the bench. "We can talk about this—"

"Let me go," Polly wept. "We can't fix this, Sam. It's broken for ever."

"It doesn't have to be—"

"I don't want this," Polly said. "You in London, me here. Making arrangements to see each other, and then cancelling when other stuff comes up. Waiting by the phone . . . I can't do it. Don't you understand?"

"But I'm falling in love with you," Sam said desperately.

His words hardened Polly's heart. *Love is nothing but trouble*, she thought savagely. *People in love just hurt each other more.*

"Let's be honest and end it here," she said. "Goodbye, Sam."

He let go of her arm as if she had slapped him. Unable to bear the look on his face, Polly ran for the park gate, wiping the tears from her eyes.

Her breath came in loud, ragged gasps as she pounded down the quiet street, her scarf flying, her legs pumping. Where was she going? She didn't know.

157

She didn't care. She just wanted to run and run until she fell to the ground and stopped feeling the pain. Anything was better than this.

Sam's face would haunt her for ever. The betrayal in his eyes, the tears on his cheeks.

She swerved away from the streetlights, aiming instead for the darkness of the lanes that wound up from Heartside Bay into the hills. The further she ran, the darker it became. Streetlights were few and far between now, which suited her fine. She wanted to run into the darkest place she could find, and hide there for ever. Her knees shook. Her lungs felt as if they were going to burst. She plunged on.

The sea gleamed beyond the town, lit by the pure white light of the moon. Now her eyes were accustomed to it, everything felt as bright as day.

As she swerved round a corner, she realized dimly that someone was running towards her at full speed. Head down, headphones in, black wires trailing down the front of a pale hoodie. He hadn't seen her. He was going to crash right into her. She saw all this as if from a distance, as if it was about to happen to someone else, someone who wasn't her at all.

The jogger glanced up just in time.

"Whoa!" he said, skidding to a halt. Stones flew up from beneath his trainers.

Polly wobbled in shock, lost her footing and staggered to the side of the road, where her legs folded beneath her like a deckchair and she sat, suddenly, on the verge. She buried her pounding head in her hands.

Of all the people she could have bumped into tonight, she thought in despair, why did it have to be Ollie?

Ollie pulled his headphones from his ears. His blond hair looked wet and dark in the moonlight. "Polly?" he said in astonishment. "Are you OK?"

Polly peeped at him through her fingers, struggling to breathe. Now she had stopped running, her legs were agony. *I probably look like a lunatic*, she thought hysterically.

She felt him sit on the verge beside her. "I thought you were a ghost, looming out of nowhere like that. What's happened? What are you doing up here?'"

She scrubbed at her eyes, which felt gritty and red. "Escaping," she mumbled.

His eyebrows lifted, mystified. "From what? A hungry lion?"

She was still trembling from head to foot. "My life," she said in despair.

"What's wrong with your life?"

"Everything," she groaned.

"Hey, hey, don't cry," Ollie said, putting his arm round her. "Talk to me."

The kindness of the gesture made Polly cry all over again. Burying her face in his warm fleecy front, she sobbed and hiccupped and blurted out the whole story about Sam: how they had met, how they had lost and then found each other again. And how it was over already, before it had properly begun. She was beyond caring what Ollie thought of her as she sobbed all over his hoodie.

"He's probably congratulating himself on escaping," she wept. "I'm neurotic, obsessive, insecure – everything that Sam's not. I know it's better this way. So why does it hurt so much?'

"Just because we know something's right, doesn't make it easy," Ollie said over her head. "And as for Sam congratulating himself – I don't think so. Look at you, Polly. You're bright, funny, original. Any guy would be lucky to have you. This is totally Sam's loss. He's not good enough for you."

Polly punched Ollie weakly in the shoulder. "You were horrible to him tonight."

"That's because he's a pompous idiot," Ollie said promptly. "I mean, goat's cheese and rocket pizza? Are rockets even edible? Rockets should stick to what they know: powering through the universe, full of astronauts."

"It's a great pizza combination, actually," Polly said, wiping her eyes.

"Sure it is," said Ollie. "If you're a hungry astronaut with an allergy to nice normal cows."

Polly laughed in spite of herself. "You're pretty original yourself, you know."

"Aw," said Ollie, resting his head against hers. "That's the nicest thing you've ever said to me."

It probably was, Polly realized. She had spent so many years bickering with Ollie, teasing him, winding him up, desperate for him to notice her but desperate for him not to know how she really felt about him. She could hardly believe he was here with her, in the moonlight, sitting on the side of the road. His arm felt warm on her shoulders, like it was meant to be there.

"How was the film anyway?" she asked, sniffing.

Ollie pulled a face. "We didn't go. Lila was so mad at me she left pretty much straight after you did, leaving me to sort out the bill. It wasn't our best date ever."

The atmosphere changed at the mention of Lila's name. Polly suddenly felt guilty sitting out here in the dark with Ollie's arm round her – as if they were Eve and Max sneaking around behind Rhi's back. Confusing feelings threatened to overwhelm her.

"We should try and get along better," she said into the silence, trying to move things along. "You know. For Lila's sake."

Ollie abruptly took his arm away. "I've always been nice to you," he said, shoving his hands into his pockets. "You're the one who won't lay off the dumb-jock jokes."

Polly groped for a response. "You're the one who compared my dress to a curtain!"

"Only after you said my brain was made of marshmallows." His voice sounded strangely tight.

He stood up and brushed his joggers down. "Why am I even sitting here like this with you? You should run back to your brainy boyfriend in the park. You two are made for each other."

Polly was cut to the quick. Where was his anger coming from? Barely seconds ago, she had been resting her head on his shoulder. Now he was looking at her like she was mud.

"Thanks for nothing," she managed. "Oh, and remind me never to spill the contents of my soul at the feet of a football player again!"

"Don't tell me." Ollie slotted his headphones back into his ears. "You think I'll kick them into the back of the net."

"You just did!" Polly shouted. "Are you going to pull your jumper over your head now and run around the pitch like a dumb gorilla howling at the moon?"

"Ug!" Ollie grunted, beating his chest and capering around on the moonlit road in front of her. "Ug ug! That's me, Polly. All brawn and no brain. Ug!"

Polly covered her ears. She hated him so much right then. "Go away!" she screamed. "Sam's right about you. You're . . . you're stupid and lazy and . . . and. . ."

"You deserve each other," Ollie said bitterly.

He jogged away into the darkness with a sarcastic wave.

Polly felt worse than ever. It was as if those precious moments of kindness had never happened. Those moments when it had just been the two of them against the world.

This had truly been the evening from hell.

TWENTY

Polly didn't sleep well. She heard the clock downstairs chime every hour from two until eight. Every time she tried to go to sleep, the horrible images of the previous evening threatened to drown her. Ollie at the restaurant. Sam in the park. Ollie in the moonlight, looking at her like he hated her. What was she doing? How would she get through this?

She staggered out of bed at ten and had the hottest shower she could bear. Lobster pink and wrapped in a massive towel, she sat on the floor of her bedroom and wept until her eyes were as pink as her skin. Then she blew her nose and opened her wardrobe. Her dad had texted to confirm that he would meet her on the beach at twelve. There was nothing her mum could do about it. Now all she had to do was struggle with her daily battle of what to wear. It was too much.

All she could think about was Sam's unhappy face in the park, and Ollie's moonlit back as he jogged away from her in the dark. Sam, Ollie, Sam, Ollie. She wanted to scream.

Her phone buzzed.

I'm sorry. Please talk to me, Polly.
My heart is broken.
S xx

He even got his punctuation right, Polly thought dully. No one ever bothered with punctuation in texts. No one but Sam, apparently.

No sooner had Polly read the message than another one appeared.

We only have three days left.
I want to enjoy them with you.
Life is too short for this. Love S xx

No boy had ever texted that word to her before. Polly

wavered, remembering the magic of Sam's kisses. She put down her phone and looked back at her half-tidied wardrobe. Then she burst into fresh tears and threw herself across the bed, burying her head in her pillow. She couldn't cope with any of it today.

Her mother put her head round the door. She was across the room in two strides, holding Polly and stroking her hair.

"Oh, my baby. What's the matter? Is it Sam? Is it your dad?"

"Sam's leaving," Polly wept. "His parents are getting a divorce and his mum's moving to London and he's going with her. I can't bear it, I can't bear it. . ."

"I'm so sorry, love," her mother said, holding her tightly. "Love can be cruel. When your father left—"

"Shut up about Dad," said Polly savagely, pressing her hands to her ears. "Just *shut up*!"

She shoved her mother away and flew off the bed, pressing her back to the wall, trying to put as much distance between them as she could. Anger and grief poured out of her in a tidal wave.

"I hate how you are about Dad all the time," Polly shouted.

Her mother's face was chalk-white with shock. "Polly, I—"

"Everyone leaves!" Polly's lungs felt like they were in a vice. She picked up a picture frame and threw it across the room. There was the sound of breaking glass. "Everyone leaves me. Parents ruin *everything*!"

It was the strangest sensation, seeing her own mother cry.

"Polly baby, I'm so sorry. . . I had no idea you felt like this. . . I just want to protect you. . ."

The shattering picture frame had punctured something in Polly. The anger left her, seeping away like poison draining from a wound. She felt bone tired but determined. Her mother had to understand.

"I want to see Dad," she said simply. "And he wants to see me. That's never going to change, Mum. You have to learn to get along with him for my sake."

Tears ran down her mother's cheeks. "I'm so sorry," she repeated, reaching unsteadily for the tissues by Polly's bed. "I've got it all wrong, haven't I? Of course you must see your dad. I . . . will try my best not to interfere any more. Now dry your eyes.

You're meeting him at twelve, aren't you? We don't have much time."

Polly sat on the bed and let her mother pull things from her wardrobe and lay them out for her to choose. She felt calmer. Her heart was still in pieces, but something else felt as if it was maybe starting to heal.

She chose a vintage gold blouse and a pair of bright teal jeans. Then she grabbed a thick oversized cardigan.

"When do you think you'll be back?" asked her mother as Polly headed for the front door.

"I'll call you," said Polly firmly. Her mother would have to be content with that.

The sun was out, feeling warm on her shoulders, and as she walked into town she realized that she had made a decision about America. Perhaps it was her argument with her mum which had unlocked the answer. Whatever the reason, it was a good feeling, knowing what she wanted to do with her life again.

Her dad was waiting by the seafront, perched on the seawall with two ice-cream cones in his hands.

"Love the colour combination," he said, kissing her

cheek while holding the ice creams precariously out to the side. "You have such a great eye for clothes, Polly-Dolly. How have you been?"

If only you knew, thought Polly. "Not bad," she said aloud.

Her father gave her the ice cream. "Organic and local," he said happily. "Even the cone is made a short way down the coast. It makes it so much more special, don't you think? I know it's bad to eat ice cream before lunch, but I couldn't resist."

They walked side by side on the beach, listening to the gulls and watching the waves curl and crash on the sand. Polly tried not to think of Sam's boat bobbing out there among the scudding sails on the blue horizon.

Her father was enthusing about his farm and all the plans he had for the land. "When you farm biodynamically, Polly, you harness everything so that it works in harmony—"

Polly interrupted him. "How far is the farm from the beach?"

"About a twenty-minute drive," he said, smiling. "And what a beach it is. It's a little wilder than here, with no town or anything like that. But it's so beautiful. The dunes stretch for miles."

Polly dug her toes in the cool sand. "I've decided I want to live with you," she said. "But don't tell anyone yet, OK? I need to pick the right moment to break the news to Mum."

When would the right moment be? she wondered. She would have to tell Lila as well. She didn't know which would be worse. But she had made her decision, so she knew that she would find a way. It was time for a fresh start. This was the perfect opportunity to start again.

Her father's face was a picture of delight. "That's wonderful news! We are going to have such a great time, building our life on the farm. It'll be like the old days!"

"No it won't," said Polly. She smiled, wanting him to know that she didn't mind. "Because these are *new* days, Dad. I want to remember that."

TWENTY-ONE

By Saturday morning, Polly still hadn't found the courage to tell her mother she wanted to move to the States in a week's time.

She and her dad had planned everything yesterday afternoon, and Polly's head was buzzing with information: about school, and the farm, and the store, and the recycled clothes she would make to sell, and the website they would build together. But every time she built herself up to explaining her plans to her mother, she lost her nerve.

Her mum was trying her best to be nice about her dad, Polly noticed. She hadn't said anything bad about him since their fight the previous day, and was bending over backwards to keep Polly happy. She had even said, "If he ever wants to pick you up from here, tell him that's fine. I could maybe put the kettle on so we can all talk together."

Polly could see how hard it was for her mum to change years of behaviour overnight. She dreaded to think how she would react to the much more dramatic news that Polly was planning to emigrate for good.

That morning, her mum had made a cake for them to share over a cup of tea before she went to work. Her mum wasn't the world's greatest baker, and the cake was burned around the edges and a little dry, but Polly appreciated the effort. It made her feel doubly guilty about her plans.

"When's your dad moving into his farm then?" her mum asked, slicing the cake.

Polly wondered if her mother could see the guilt in her eyes. "I'm not sure," she mumbled, and took a bite from the cake to save herself from saying anything else. There was never going to be a good time for breaking news like this, she realized. She would just have to be brave and jump right in.

"I'm sure he'll make it very special," said her mum. "He was always good at things like that."

Polly swallowed the cake. It made her throat even drier.

"Mum?" she said hesitantly.

Her phone buzzed in her pocket. With a wave of relief, she checked the screen and pushed away from the table. Her news could wait.

"It's Lila," she said. "I'd better answer it."

"Send her my love," said her mum as Polly hurried out of the kitchen, lifting her phone to her ear.

"Hey."

"Hey yourself! We haven't spoken since the apple juice thing. Boy, what a disaster! I was so angry with Ollie, I stormed out of the restaurant not long after you did. Remind me never to sort out a double date again," Lila sighed. "Listen, do you want to help me throw an end-of-half-term beach party?"

Pain sliced through Polly as she remembered meeting Sam after the last beach party they'd had. Was that only a week ago?

"The weather's still great," Lila went on, "so I thought we could go back to the secret cove tomorrow afternoon, make a campfire, put together a really great playlist, all the stuff we did before. Only we could make it *extra* special this time by doing some proper food. After last week, I never want to eat another marshmallow again."

A strange thought struck Polly. If this party went ahead, it wouldn't just mark the end of half-term. It could be her leaving party as well. Her dad was only planning to be in the UK for a few more days, and she would be joining him on the plane to San Francisco next week.

Lila was still talking enthusiastically.

"We could do baked potatoes, although we'd have to put them in the fire as soon as we built it – they take so long to cook, but they are so worth it with beans and cheese and other yummy things on top."

"We could do bananas and chocolate in foil too," Polly found herself saying.

"Brilliant!" Lila said at once. "Will you meet me in town to get the stuff this afternoon?"

Downstairs, Polly heard the front door click shut and the car starting up as her mum left for work. She hated the feeling of relief. She would tell her mum tonight, she promised herself. She would make herself do it.

Half an hour later she was standing with Lila outside the supermarket.

"OK, so I've called everyone and they can all make it tomorrow afternoon," said Lila as they collected a trolley.

"Even Eve and Max?" Polly asked.

"Obviously not them," said Lila, rolling her eyes in return. "They aren't invited. Rhi hasn't heard a thing from either of them all week. They're probably loved up on Eve's dad's boat right now." She glared in the general direction of the harbour. "I was going to ask Max to do the music like last week, but hello? Who wants anything to do with the guy now? I'll ask Ollie instead."

Polly's heart gave its customary flutter at the mention of Ollie's name. She wondered if he'd told Lila about their moonlit fight on Thursday evening.

"What's Ollie's music like?"

"Terrible," Lila grinned. "But more party-like than mine. I have a list of what we need, let's go."

They moved through the supermarket aisles, discussing the party as they went along. Polly started to feel quite excited as they piled bananas and dark-chocolate bars into their arms.

"So how's the gorgeous Sam anyway?" Lila asked,

reaching up for a box of silver foil to add to the growing pile in the trolley.

Polly's heart gave a jump. She hadn't thought about Sam for several hours because she'd had too much else on her mind. But now he was back inside her head, his hazel eyes full of tears and his voice pleading with her to talk about it.

"That's over," she said as steadily as she could. "He's moving to London next week. We decided to call it quits."

Lila's mouth fell open. "What? But you guys only just got together!"

"Tell me about it," Polly sighed. "He told me on Thursday night. After . . . you know. The restaurant."

"But what happened?"

Polly told Lila about Sam's parents getting divorced, and his internship with the politician. She knew this was the moment to tell her best friend about her plans to move to America as well, but she couldn't face it.

You're a coward, Polly Nelson, she told herself with a sigh.

"Did you think of asking Sam to stay, and forget about the internship?' Lila asked.

Polly shook her head. "Politics is his life. He wants to change the world so badly. I can't stand in his way."

Lila looked troubled. "You're right. Politics will always come first for Sam, won't they? The protest march, now this. That's not good for anyone, being second best."

Polly frowned. "What do you mean?"

Lila fiddled with her hair. "If I tell you something," she said at last, "will you swear not to tell anyone else?"

"You can tell me anything," Polly answered, intrigued now.

Lila pushed her swinging brown hair out of her eyes. "It's Ollie," she confided. "Things aren't going all that great with him and me at the moment. He's still a lovely guy, but . . . I don't know. It's like the spark is fading between us. We seem to argue a lot, and it's like he doesn't smile at me as much as he used to."

Polly was glad she was holding on to the trolley. Her legs felt strangely shaky. "Seriously?"

Lila nodded. "It's the weirdest thing, but I always feel like I come second in Ollie's life."

Polly brought the trolley to a halt. "You knew he was committed to his football when you started going out with him," she pointed out.

"I thought it was the football at first." Lila absently opened one of the bars of chocolate in the trolley and bit into it. "But I'm getting the sensation that this is really about something else. Or should I say, some*one* else. I think he's got secret feelings for another girl that he's hiding from me."

Polly felt sick. "Secret feelings about who?"

"I don't know," Lila said. Then she shook her head like she was clearing water from her ears and smiled at Polly. "Listen to me, banging on. Like you need to hear any of this when you've got romance problems of your own. Sorry, Pol. Ignore me." She squeezed Polly's arm, her big blue eyes wide and serious. "I never want anything to come between us, OK? Boys, friends, none of it. You're too important to me."

Polly felt a terrible urge to climb inside the shopping trolley and hide among the potatoes they'd bought. How could she even *think* of leaving Heartside when Lila needed her so much? It would break her friend's heart. And Ollie—

No. She wouldn't think about Ollie right now. Going to California was the right decision. Wasn't it?

They took the shopping back to Polly's house because it was closer to the secret cove for transporting the party stuff the following day. Their bags were heavy, and Polly had to concentrate on holding them in such a way that they didn't cut off the circulation in her fingers. Her head was full to bursting with everything as Lila chattered on about the next day's party. She wished she could go somewhere quiet and dark and really think it all through.

"Psst," said Lila suddenly.

Sam was waiting by the gate. Polly's stomach flip-flopped.

"Can we go to yours?" she said in panic.

"You guys need to talk," said Lila, giving her a gentle shove. "Sam's leaving in a few days. Make the most of the time you have left. I'll see you tomorrow at eleven to get the stuff down to the cove."

Before Polly could protest, Lila had smiled at Sam, put her share of the shopping bags on the pavement outside Polly's house, and jogged away down the road.

Sam was looking extremely gorgeous in the blustery

sunshine, tall and broad-shouldered with bright wind-blown colour in his cheeks. Polly could feel her resolve melting as she looked at him.

"Hey," Sam said.

"Hey yourself," she said.

They stared at each other in silence.

"I wanted to say—" he began.

"I'm really—" Polly said at the same time.

They stopped, and laughed a little uncertainly.

"So how are you?" Sam asked.

Polly pointed at the bulging bags on the pavement. "There's a party tomorrow at the beach. Lila and I went shopping."

That's not even an answer to his question, she thought hopelessly. Why was she so bad at stuff like this?

"I'm sorry I upset you last night," he said. "I didn't know how to tell you I was leaving. I guess it was never going to be easy."

"I guess not," Polly mumbled, staring hard at the shopping bags.

"Polly, please look at me."

She felt his hand slide into hers. She looked up at

him. Then somehow she was in his arms and he was kissing her, stroking her hair and hugging her and kissing her again.

"I'm sorry," he whispered against her tear-streaked cheeks.

She clung to him. "I know. I'm sorry too."

Holding her hard against him, Sam looked down at her. "What are you thinking?" he said.

"This is going to end in a few days," Polly said. Given her plans for America, this was even truer than Sam knew. "But it's right, what you said in your text. Life's too short not to enjoy what we can."

He kissed her again. "And we're really going to enjoy it, OK?" he said when he released her. "We'll go out tonight, somewhere really special, just you and me. And we can talk and be with each other and laugh and do all the things we love doing together."

"Sounds good," said Polly through her tears.

And it did.

TWENTY-TWO

The sun was warm against the cliff. Polly could feel the heat through her dress as she leaned against the rocks with Sam's arm round her and a bottle of cold juice in her hand. The remains of a cheesy potato nestled in fire-blackened foil beside her. Sam clinked bottles and smiled into her eyes.

"Having fun?" he said.

"The most," Polly sighed. If she closed her eyes she could feel the sun warming her eyelids. She felt loose and calm, full and happy and loved. It was a combination that didn't come along very often.

Ollie's dance music echoed and boomed off the rocks surrounding the cove, and there were people dancing everywhere. One or two braver guys had gone swimming, and were now chasing each other across the beach with handfuls of sand.

Rhi was laughing so much with Lila that she sprayed half a chocolate banana over her T-shirt. The chocolatey mess only made her and Lila laugh even more as they danced wildly to the music.

What a difference a week makes, Polly thought, remembering how distraught Rhi had been on the boat trip. She hadn't seen Max since then, and as for Eve. . . She shuddered as she remembered Eve's attempted seduction of Sam at Heartwell Manor. It was hard to imagine going back to school tomorrow. It felt as if she had lived a whole new life since the last time she set foot in the classroom.

Polly realized that Sam hadn't been sitting beside her for a while. Turning her head, she surveyed the rounded, bumpy-looking sandcastle he was making.

"What do you think?" he asked.

"What is it?"

"A seal, of course. The small bump's its head" – he patted the rounded shape to demonstrate – "and the rest is its body under the water."

Now that he'd said it, Polly could see the resemblance. He had even added stripes in the sand for the seal's whiskers.

"Brilliant," she said. "Now can we stomp on it?"

"You can't stomp on a seal!" Sam objected.

Polly jumped to her feet. "Watch me,' she said teasingly.

"That's vandalism!" Sam protested, grabbing her round the waist and pulling her down on to the sand with him.

"OK, so I'm a vandal," Polly said, smiling up at him. "What's my sentence?"

"The longest kiss that you can stand," Sam answered. "Starting now."

In the middle of their kiss, Polly heard a strange sound. She twisted her head and stared at the rocks behind them.

"Can you hear that?"

"All I can hear is the beating of my heart," Sam announced.

Polly gave him a shove in the chest. "Seriously," she said, grinning. "Listen."

"*Help! Help us!*"

"That sounds like it's coming from inside the cliff," said Sam.

It did. Polly got to her feet and rested her ear against the rock. The shout was still faint, but clearer.

"*Help us!*"

"They must be in the caves," Polly said, realizing. "These cliffs are riddled with them. Whoever it is sounds like they're in trouble."

"How do you get inside?" asked Sam, staring up at the golden cliff face.

Polly grabbed his hand and pulled him down the edge of the cove. "Here," she said, pointing at a small black entrance near the water. "You can only get inside when the tide goes out." A nasty thought struck her. "The tide's going to turn soon. Whoever's inside needs to get out, fast."

Sam pulled a torch from his back pocket and flicked it on. "Be prepared," he said, smiling at Polly's surprised face. "That's something you learn as a scout, and keep learning as a sailor."

The cave was low to begin with, dank and dripping. Polly had never been inside before. She was glad to have Sam with her, his comforting bulk wriggling through the rocky passages in front of her. The sand was wet for the first few metres, then grew drier as they rose above sea level.

"Help!"

This time the shout ended on a sob of panic.

"We're coming!" Sam shouted back.

There was the sound of scuffling somewhere up ahead. Polly held on tightly to Sam's hand, her free hand brushing up against the damp rocks.

"We are going to be able to get out of here," she said a little weakly. "Right?"

Sam checked the luminous face on his watch. "We have a little while until the tide turns. Provided we find these guys, we'll be out in plenty of time."

They walked on. The light from outside barely penetrated this deep inside the cliff. In the gleam of Sam's torch, Polly saw messages scrawled on the rock faces, hearts and dates carved everywhere she looked. Heartside Bay is the capital of love inside *and* out, she thought.

The tunnel widened out into a cave. Sam's torch lit it up in its entirety, high-roofed and bone dry save for a small spring trickling clear, cold water in one corner.

The perfect hiding place, Polly thought, gazing around in wonder. This was the kind of cave that smugglers dreamed of.

"Oh thank *God*!"

Someone threw themselves out of the shadows, clutching at Sam's sleeve with a set of long, grubby fingers tipped in chipped red nail polish. A dirty, dusty figure with sand in her tangled red hair staggered into the torchlight, holding her hand up to shade her eyes from the bright light.

"Sam! Polly! I thought we were going to be in here *for ever*," Eve whimpered, weeping uncontrollably. "Max's stupid torch went out and we couldn't find our phones in the dark and—"

"It was your fault we came in here in the first place," Max complained, slouching into the light of the torch behind Eve. His hair was covered in silvery spiders' webs and his jumper was torn. "You said it would be romantic. If crawling around in the pitch dark is your idea of romance, then I'm with the wrong girl."

"Oh, like you didn't think it was the best idea you'd ever heard?" Eve snapped, a flash of her usual sharp-clawed self emerging through the tangled hair and frightened eyes. "Get us out of here before I murder him, Sam, will you? We've been shouting for *hours*."

Eve's tone of voice suggested that all this was somehow Polly and Sam's fault for taking such a long time in coming to the rescue.

"Fine," Sam said equably. "We'll leave you then, shall we? The next lot will probably get in after the tides have turned, so if you can hang around until the morning for a more suitable rescue party. . ."

Polly giggled at the look on Eve's face.

"The exit's this way," Sam sighed, relenting.

It was typical of Eve not even to thank them, Polly thought as they negotiated the tunnels sloping back down towards the water level. Sam flicked his torch off as the daylight grew stronger. Polly could hear Eve and Max behind them, bickering like angry wasps the whole way.

"Next time I want to hang out in a cave I'll join a speleological society."

"Next time you want to hang out in a cave, I'll wall it up and leave you there!"

They all crawled out of the cave mouth, wading through the inches of water which had started gathering among the rocks as the tide started to creep back into shore. Eve was an even more pitiful sight in the sunshine. Her make-up was streaked down her face and there was a long ladder in her tights. Polly knew it was bad to enjoy her enemy's misfortune, but she allowed herself a private grin.

Lila was the first to explode with laughter as the dusty couple sidled up the beach towards the campfire.

"You two are the best thing I've seen in ages," she said in delight. "Halloween isn't for another six or seven months, Eve."

"Shut up," Eve hissed, her shoulders hunched and defensive. "I know I look like hell, OK?"

"Go ahead and laugh," Max added sourly. He snatched up a can of Coke and drained it in one go, wiping his mouth and smearing the cave dirt sideways across his face. It just made the crowd laugh even more.

"Oh, we will," Ollie assured him, grinning.

"Cut them some slack, guys," said Rhi, surprising everyone.

Polly saw that Max had the decency to blush as Rhi approached him looking calm and serious. Eve folded her arms more tightly and stared at the sky.

"They look like they've had a tough time," Rhi went on. She considered Max's dirty face. "I used to think you were handsome," she said in surprise. "Now I realize you're just a clown."

Max silently swigged the rest of his Coke, and stared at the sand in defeat.

Good for you Rhi, Polly thought. *That took guts.* She needed guts like that to break the news to everyone that she was going to America.

Or did she?

Like the horizon after a storm, something started coming into focus in Polly's mind. She stared at her friends, at the campfire, at Ollie laughing with his buddies. At the way the sun striped the sand and the cliffs glowed like gold in the afternoon light. She felt Sam's hand in hers, and the ridged sand under her bare feet. She felt rooted, suddenly, like she hadn't felt in a very long time.

"Oh, and Eve? You and Max can both stay for the rest of the party," Rhi added, breaking into Polly's whirling thoughts.

Eve stopped staring at the sky. "What?"

"I'll never forgive you," Rhi said, looking steadily

at Eve, "but I can't keep avoiding you. So let's all just move on."

Eve brushed fussily at her clothes to avoid looking at Rhi's face. "Look at me," she grumbled. "I'll have to go home and shower first."

Max gave the first real smile Polly had seen all day. "Oh, that's easily fixed," he drawled.

Before Eve could react, he had scooped her into his broad arms and was sprinting towards the sea.

"Don't you dare!" Eve shrieked in horror, fighting to get away from him. "Max Holmes, if you—"

There was a splash as Max tipped Eve into the freezing waves. After a split second of shocked silence, there was a piercing scream of rage.

"This ... tank ... is ... CASHMERE!" Eve roared, belting Max around every part of his body that she could reach.

"That's got to hurt," Lila observed.

"Max will get over it," said Rhi. She laughed. "I don't know about that tank, though."

The last piece fell into place for Polly. She had been running away instead of facing things, she realized. Her life was here, with her friends. There was plenty of time ahead to make a life in fashion, not to mention long vacations with her dad in California, helping him with the store and the website. She could have all the good things this way, both at home and in the States.

Suddenly she couldn't wait to get started.

Heartside isn't perfect, she realized, wiping the tears of laughter from her eyes and resting her head on Sam's shoulder. *But it's home.*

TWENTY-THREE

"Let's take a walk," Sam said in Polly's ear.

The tide really was creeping back to shore now, closing the gap between the sands of the secret cove and the town beach. Polly let Sam lead her towards the path, the sound of music and laughter and Eve's screams following them on the air.

"You're going in a minute," she said as they walked. "Aren't you?"

Sam indicated the way the water was creeping back in to shore. "I have to go with the tide. But my boat's moored a little way up the beach. We still have time."

They walked around the whole of the beach, hand in hand. Gulls wheeled overhead, screaming and swooping and squabbling over squashed and crumpled bags of chips left lying along the harbour wall. Sandcastles, some as ambitious as whole towns and others simple turrets of sand decorated with shells, were starting to leak back into the sea as the tide brought them gently crumbling down, leaving nothing behind to show they had been there at all. The town clock chimed over the noise of the waves, solid and reassuring.

They looped back the way they had come, and stopped by the sweeping outcrop that pointed its long rocky finger at Kissing Island. Polly recognized his boat, now bobbing at anchor just off the shoreline.

"It was here, wasn't it?" Sam said. "Our campfire?"

Polly could see their little driftwood fire in her mind's eye, and bright and flickering as if it were still there. "Pretty much," she said.

He shaded his eyes against the setting sun, pointing out to sea. "And your rock was that one, right?"

Polly's throat was filling up. She nodded as tears spilled down her cheeks.

"Don't cry, mermaid," he said with a smile, brushing her tears away with his fingers. "Too many tears stop your scales from shining."

Polly sniffed hard. "Stay," she blurted.

"I can't," he said regretfully. "This London internship is too good an opportunity. I'm going to be the change I want to see, Polly. And it all starts here."

He took her cheeks in his hands, just as he had that first afternoon, and kissed her tenderly. Polly stood on tiptoes with her arms around his neck and her fingers stroking the soft bristly hairs on the nape of his neck. She loved the way Sam had opened her eyes to the wider world. But Lila was right. She would always be second best to Sam's ambitions. And as much as she admired him for his political passion, she deserved to come first.

This was OK, she realized. They were young. Time would heal it all, leaving nothing but sunny memories. She would always be grateful to Sam for that. And she would never forget him.

He kissed her one last time, then waded out to his boat, which was tugging and straining at its anchor. "Stay in touch!" he called as he leaped aboard. "And make sure you vote for me one day!"

It's a fitting end, Polly thought, watching through her tears as the wind filled Sam's sails. She remembered the first time she had seen him and his cherry-coloured jumper and the white lines of his boat on this very shoreline. *A perfect circle.*

Polly watched and waved until Sam was out of sight. Then she turned back towards the town. She would go home, she decided. She wasn't in the mood for any more partying.

Ollie stood a little way up the beach. He raised his hand as Polly approached.

"Hey," said Polly, stopping in surprise. "What are you doing here?"

Ollie shrugged. "The party's over. So I thought I'd come and see how you were doing." He gazed over Polly's shoulder at the little dot on the waves that maybe was and maybe wasn't Sam's white boat. "So he's definitely going to London?"

Polly nodded.

"Too bad," said Ollie. "I may not have liked the guy, but I wasn't the one going out with him. You were. So." He scratched his ear. "Are you OK?"

Polly thought about the last time Ollie had tried to cheer her up, out in that moonlit lane on Thursday night before it had all gone wrong.

"I'm fine," she said honestly. "It hurts a bit, but I'll live."

"Kind of like ripping off a plaster," Ollie said, nodding. "Fast is best."

Polly giggled. "Are you comparing my relationship with Sam to a plaster?"

"Yeah," Ollie agreed. "One of those big ones that stick to the hairs on your legs and hurt like hell unless you soak them off in the shower first."

Polly wanted to hug him. "Sheesh," she said, grinning. "You really have the scope of the thing, don't you?"

"Don't take the mick," he said, with a lopsided smile.

She didn't want to, Polly realized. Ollie's plaster comparison was the perfect description. Funny too.

"You always know how to make me feel better," she said wonderingly.

He looked disbelieving. "I had the opposite effect on that hill last week."

"I wasn't at my best last week," Polly confessed.

"Me neither."

He ran his hands through his blond hair, looking

up at her from beneath his eyebrows in that sweet, quirky way he had. And there it was. The pinging feeling in her gut was back. She had liked Sam, but she had always – *always* – liked Ollie more.

"Friends again?" he said.

Polly nodded. "Friends again."

"You know," he said, scuffing at the sand with the toe of his trainer, "I have a feeling me and Lila are at the plaster-ripping stage."

Polly suddenly felt shy. "That's too bad."

He looked up again, frowning. "It is?"

Don't make an idiot of yourself, Polly ordered herself.

"Well," she fumbled. "It's too bad if *you* think it's too bad."

He quirked his mouth. "And if I *don't* think it's too bad, too bad?"

It was impossible to get too serious with Ollie around. Grinning at Polly's laughter, Ollie slung his arm round her shoulders and gave her a squeeze.

"Shall we go find the others?" he asked, looking down at her.

Polly barely heard the question. She had seen something in his eyes. . .

She remembered Lila's words.

I think he's got secret feelings for another girl that he's hiding from me.

She had feelings for Ollie, she knew that much.

Was it possible that Ollie had feelings for her too?

"Hey, you," Ollie said gently. His arm was still there. "Are we walking or standing still?"

"Walking," said Polly after a moment. "We're walking."

This wasn't entirely true. Inside, she was flying.